I0831179

STEEL AGAINST THE DAMNED

THE DAMNED – BOOK ONE

STEEL AGAINST THE DAMNED

GUY D. STAPP

URGANOTH PRESS LLC

"Desert Fang" first appeared as "The Bad Blade" in *Written in Blood* (Storytelling Collective, 2024), and has been heavily revised for this collection.

Published by Urganoth Press

www.urganothpress.com

ISBN 979-8-9940682-2-9 (hardback)

ISBN 979-8-9940682-0-5 (paperback)

ISBN 979-8-9940682-1-2 (e-book)

Cover art by Alejandro Colucci

Copyediting by Gary Budden

Proofreading by Matt Webster-Moore

For my beautiful wife

whose encouragement means everything.

You are my best friend.

CONTENTS

FORBIDDEN FEAST

PROLOGUE

Branoc hurried toward the sounds of violence, his torch sputtering as shadows flinched from its light.

The boy was still unaccustomed to his gambeson, the padded cloth making him clumsy and hot. He wondered again how the Silvermen—*Galani Yidwyr*, he reminded himself—could move so swiftly in armor twice as heavy.

Struggling to match Branoc's pace, the seer hunched beneath the low ceiling of the side passage. He dared not leave the old man behind in the dark.

Reaching a dead end, they entered a chamber littered with yellowed and cracked bones. The three Silvermen knelt within a circle of salt drawn around a hairless creature with pallid gray skin, long claws, and a beastly maw.

Steel bracers and mail shirts gleamed faintly over the Yidwyrs' scarred leathers. Two of them wore silver chains coiled around their middles, but the third's waist was bare. His chain was wrapped around the creature's arms and torso. Its severed head had been set back upon its shoulders, the silver links dangling from its open jaws.

Erigan, their leader, pressed a silver coin into the creature's brow, uttering ominous words in a language the boy could not understand. They echoed around the chamber, filling him with dread.

The chains wrapped around the creature began to glow—subtle at first, and then white hot. The smell of burning flesh tinged with a sharp metallic tang assaulted the boy's nose. Blue flames limned the creature's hide, which cracked and flaked before being blown away by a wind that touched none of the men.

A moment later, nothing was left but the silver chain and the coin amid the scattered ashes and scorched outline of the creature.

Erigan ceased his invocation, and the Silvermen murmured in unison, "By our oath and silver purged, let no power restore this fiend."

Branoc reached for the coin, but it burned his fingers. He dropped it, hissing through his teeth.

Erigan snatched up the coin and wrapped the chain around his waist.

"What language was that?" the boy asked.

Erigan cuffed his ear. "That is for dawdling." To the others he said, "Let us go. This one strayed off on its own, but we can still follow the trail to its pack."

Branoc's ear was still stinging when they reached the main passage they had been following before, but the boy could not resist asking questions any longer. "I don't understand the ritual," he said to the seer. "The creature was already dead. Why bother with it?"

As if weighing what knowledge he had earned, the old man studied the boy.

Branoc's brow furrowed. Though only a thirteen-year-old apprentice, not a true Galani Yidwyr, he was putting himself in just as much danger as they all were.

"The binding ritual is necessary to destroy the ghoul's soul as well as its body. Otherwise, it will reform in the Idir, and it can return to plague us again."

"The Idir?" the boy asked softly. The word raised the hairs on the back of his neck.

After a moment, the seer answered. "A realm between realms, in the dreams of the ghouls' six-armed goddess—stitched together with the eternal nightmares of those devoured by her children."

Branoc was fascinated, if still frightened. "How do you know this?"

A contemplative expression settled on the seer's face. Finally, he said, "There is a tome. The Legamathan Codex. No one can study it for long without becoming corrupted. But before we understood this and sealed it deep beneath Caer Argyn, the Gwelydwyr managed to translate fragments from it. From those fragments, we learned of the Idir, how to destroy the ghouls, and other secrets not meant to be shared with young Yidwyr."

Sensing the boy's next question, the old man preempted him. "As to how the Gwelydwyr came into possession of the codex... a tale best left unspoken in this place."

It was clear the seer would say no more. After that, the group walked in silence.

His excitement having faded, the boy examined his surroundings. He trailed his fingers along the wall, the stone damp and cool to the touch. He looked down at the cobbled stones beneath his feet, feeling the weight of their depth beneath the city. Who would have laid them here, and for what purpose?

A massive vault lay at the end of the broad passage. The boy and the old man followed the Silvermen into a vast, circular chamber, its walls punctuated by archways spaced evenly around the circumference. A trail of haphazardly discarded bones, gnawed and split, pointed the way toward the arch the ghouls had taken.

As they traversed the vault, a peculiar breeze touched the boy's face, and he detected a subtle shift in their surroundings. The draft was out of place, given their distance beneath the surface, but he sensed the strangeness of it went beyond the preternatural. The earthy scent of old bones and damp stone was smothered by something more exotic like a forbidden spice. The light from their torches softened, dreamlike, and their speech slowed, almost imperceptibly.

Halting at a stone balcony, the Silvermen peered over a vast gallery swallowed by shadow. Its size could only be guessed at.

The breeze the boy had felt before intensified; the flames from their torches withered.

Closing his eyes, the seer began to chant softly in a strange tongue: "*Dyn Ythra Nef Yllath, Garanth Vael.*" His voice gathered strength with each repetition. The wind increased in defiance, whipping and shrieking around them, but the seer's chant grew bolder still.

The gale died suddenly, and the old man ceased his chant, opening his eyes. All was quiet.

One of the Silvermen extended his torch over the wall, as far as he could into the emptiness beyond the balcony, but the boy could make out no details of what lay below. The Silverman let the torch fall from his hand, and the boy leaned over the wall and followed it with his eyes. As it tumbled into the abyss, he briefly caught glimpses of a stone stair that twisted down to a descending series of barren platforms.

As the torch dropped, it revealed the giant head of a limestone statue, illuminated only for an instant as the torch plummeted past. There was something bestial about its face; but the figure was feminine, with numerous arms splayed from its torso.

Finally, the light hit the ground and extinguished.

Another light shone from below, as if in response, but this one was fey and green. They heard a short series of yipping calls originating from the same location as the weird glow. The boy's legs tensed for flight, and he groped for the dagger at his belt.

Then the light faded along with the sounds.

The Silverman who had dropped his torch lit another. "We must go down," he said. "This way." He walked in the direction of the stair.

A sudden pressure gripped Branoc's bladder, but he kept it to himself and followed the others. He didn't want them to know he was afraid.

They reached the stair and began to descend.

"Tread carefully," the seer cautioned.

After several turns of the stair, they reached a platform just above the statue's head. Now they could see a crown upon its brow, carved to resemble finger bones pointing upward. The top half of its face looked human, except for a third eye in the center of its brow, but its nose was a snout, and its mouth was full of powerful teeth protruding over its lips.

As they peered at the statue's face in the flickering torchlight, something moved in the crook of one of its six arms. Before they could get a good look, it had slipped into the shadows on the far side of the statue.

"We have found them," the seer whispered.

They continued making their way downward, catching glimpses of the statue at every turn of the stair. The dancing flames from their torches made it impossible to tell whether they were seeing movement among the statue's arms or simply shifting shadows.

Branoc could not tear his gaze away from the statue. One of its hands held a human heart, while the opposite held a femur. The next pair of hands held a primitive drum and a skull.

He swallowed. The last pair held a key and an hourglass. These last two objects unnerved him the most.

"What is it?" the boy asked, his voice unsteady.

The seer replied in a hushed tone, "That is Yam-Eshdu, the goddess of the flesh eaters."

They finally reached the bottom, where the stone goddess sat cross-legged upon a pedestal. Darkened archways in the nearby walls hinted at passages leading away from the massive chamber.

Something dropped from the statue, startling the boy. A pale shape hit the ground near its base—hunched but swift—and loped through the shadows into a waiting archway.

The three Silvermen took off after it, pausing at the portal it had entered just long enough to turn back to the seer and the boy.

"Don't let anything enter the tunnel behind us!" Erigan shouted, and then they were gone.

The old man and the boy made their way toward the portal. As they reached it, the fey light they had seen before from above shone again, this time from within the tunnel the Silvermen had entered.

Sounds of naked running feet and inhuman, guttural yipping filled the tunnel, along with the shouts and curses from the men.

There was a strangled cry, followed by a hoarse command from one of the Silvermen. "Flee! There are too many of—" The warning ended abruptly.

The fey light died. All was silent, except for the boy's ragged breathing.

They stared at each other, wide-eyed, for several heartbeats.

It was Branoc who forced himself to act first. Pulling the dagger from his belt, he shouted, "We have to help them!" He grimaced and ran into the tunnel.

"Brave little fool!" the old man cursed and charged after him down the passage. After a short span, the tunnel turned sharply, bringing them to a halt.

Blood stained the ground among the weapons and dropped torches of the Yidwyr, but there was no other sign of them, only a dead end marked with strange sigils. It was as if the tunnel had swallowed them whole.

"Where are they?" Branoc's voice shook.

The seer placed a palm upon the cold stone of the dead end. Then he removed a leatherbound tome from his satchel and flipped through its pages feverishly until he found what he was looking for. His hand trembled as he traced the sigils on the wall with his finger and compared them to the book.

Turning to the boy he said, "I fear they have been taken beyond our aid—into the Idir."

CHAPTER ONE

Dara sat cross-legged in her cushioned chair in the loft overlooking Tamir's shop, sipping mulled wine from a wooden cup. The tawny-haired thief wore soft leather boots, fitted linen trousers, and a black silk tunic with long sleeves to hide her tools.

The wooden chandelier above Tamir's worktable cast a pleasant glow, throwing shadows among the shelves that lined the walls, crowded with his precious, musty scrolls.

Her olive-skinned mentor leaned over the table, meticulously studying a parchment held flat by book-binding tools weighing down its corners. A detailed diagram of a building, with measurements neatly notated along each line, was sketched across the parchment. Judging by how low the candles burned in the chandelier, he had been quietly scrutinizing the drawing for the better part of an hour.

"Hmmm," he said finally.

She tapped her fingernails impatiently against her cup.

"Yes?" the old man inquired without looking up.

Dara sighed. "Do you think it is there or not?"

"It is the most likely spot for a hidden vault." Tamir turned his lined, bearded face toward her with a frown. "I should think it goes without saying that I do not approve of your scheme."

Dara closed her eyes and pinched the bridge of her delicate nose. "And yet, you still said it, as if I haven't heard that a hundred times before."

Tamir crossed his arms. "Robbing priests is dangerous enough, but the Giltwarden has real power. If you were to be caught..."

The old man's thought went unfinished, and he turned away from his young protégé.

"I've never been caught yet," Dara boasted. "Besides, this coinmaster is as dirty as they come. Rumor is he's spent a king's ransom on occult trinkets and esoteric tomes. If he's throwing that much coin at that foolishness, imagine what he has stashed away in that vault—no doubt siphoned from the common folk."

"If there really is a vault there, it will not be unguarded," Tamir cautioned.

The sharp rap of the brass knocker at the shop's entrance made him flinch.

Dara scoffed. "Don't fret, old man. Even if someone leaned on him, the man who sold me that diagram doesn't know who I am, or you for that matter."

He began furtively rolling up the drawing. "My dear," he said over his shoulder, "would you mind attending to our visitor while I put this away?"

She made her way down the narrow staircase, past the polished walnut counter and shelves lined with more scrolls and volumes. She threw back the bolt and opened the door. A well-dressed man stood framed in the doorway.

He wore a tan cloak and white surcoat over a blue jupon. A golden falcon was embroidered on the front of his surcoat, and a fine longsword hung from his belt. He was tall, and the loose cut of his clothes didn't hide the fact he was well-muscled.

His square jaw and lean face were cleanly shaven and his short, dark hair was neatly combed. He nodded at her, and Dara realized, belatedly, that she had failed to greet him during her silent appraisal.

"Good evening," he said and smiled crookedly. His voice was deep and sure. "I was expecting a gentleman to answer the door."

Dara arched an eyebrow, not quite smiling. "Why is that, exactly? Because a woman couldn't possibly own a shop that sells books?"

The man smiled again, this time exposing annoyingly perfect teeth. "Actually, no. Because the owner of this shop is an older gentleman named Tamir."

Tamir descended the staircase and stood beside Dara. "Ah, good evening, Sir Hughe."

"Good evening, Tamir. Were you able to acquire the book we spoke of?"

"Yes, yes. *The Four Virtues*, by Haecia. I set it aside for you somewhere..." Tamir began rummaging in the shelves.

"Ah. Here it is!" he said triumphantly, handing the volume to Hughe.

The knight opened it reverently—but Dara plucked it neatly from his hand.

She flipped through a few pages, then read aloud: "Bridling one's flesh and the tempering of passions is necessary in the pursuit of a virtuous life." She handed it back to him with a smirk. "How virtuously dull."

Hughe's smile thinned. "It is important for a knight to keep his intellect as sharp as his sword."

"Of course it is," Dara said lightly, stepping aside and folding her arms.

Hughe turned to Tamir. "How much for this copy?"

Tamir cleared his throat. "An illuminated manuscript in this condition? Why, at least forty—"

"Fifty," Dara cut in, nudging her mentor with a sly grin.

Tamir gave her a look.

"An acceptable price," Hughe said.

The knight followed the scribe back to the countertop, unhooked a pouch from his belt, and laid out the coins two at a time.

When the last silver regal clinked against the wood, Tamir nodded. He fetched a worn leather satchel from behind the counter, slid the book inside, and handed it over. "To keep it safe."

"Good evening to you both," Hughe said, then bowed his head respectfully and stepped out into the night.

The corner of Dara's lip curled into a sneer. "I don't trust him."

Tamir looked confused. "What do you mean, dear?"

"I mean, I don't think he was really here for a book. And casually throwing coin around like that?"

"What then?"

"Isn't it obvious?" she asked.

Tamir's eyebrows rose, but he said nothing.

Dara sighed in exasperation. "He's a spy. Or at least a member of the Watch. My activities have finally caught up with me. I'm sorry, Tamir. I never meant to leave a trail leading to your doorstep."

"Nonsense. That young man is the youngest son of Baron Kadugan, just recently arrived from his father's lands in the southeast. Sir Hughe is here to fulfill his yearly service in the duke's army, as must all young knights whose families hold land within a hundred leagues of the Beshan border."

Dara snatched her cloak from the peg on the wall next to the door and swirled it about her shoulders. "Well, I guess we'll see."

"Hold on—" Tamir began, but before he could take his third step, the door clanged shut behind her.

***

Dara's swift but silent steps soon brought her within sight of the "spy." She trailed him out of The Lanternway, over the river, and into Cheapside.

He moved with confidence, shoulders back, striding like a man with nothing to fear. His eyes stayed forward, ignoring the shadows where thieves or cut-throats might lurk.

Only a fool—or someone certain they were protected—would walk these streets in such a fashion.

Her forehead wrinkled in surprise as he turned into Sinners Alley.

No one was that big of a fool. Not even the Watch would have such faith in their authority. Not there. Not after dark.

She started to turn back... but curiosity compelled her.

With a quick shake of her head, she hastened to the building on the corner and found purchase in the cracks of its stone. She scrambled up to a windowsill, hauled herself onto it, and grabbed the gabled roof.

A moment later, Dara crept along in a crouch, parallel to the alley below, her soft boots padding across the shingles. With catlike grace, she crossed the narrow gaps between buildings without pause.

***

Hughe walked briskly behind the brothels and seedy taverns, his newly acquired book secured in the satchel slung over one shoulder. Its weight bounced comfortingly against his hip.

Pungent odors wafted from every crack and crevice in the alley. He pulled his cloak tighter against the chill night air and noted how dark the alley was beneath the crowded rooftops. He'd taken the straightest path. Now he questioned the decision.

"Well look at this," came a gravelly voice from the shadows to Hughe's right.

A short, scarred man in a leather jerkin stepped into a fleeting shaft of moonlight.

"Good evening to you," Hughe answered with a wary nod.

"What's in the bag?" the scarred man called from behind.

Hughe continued without answering or changing his pace.

A large pool of shadow moved up ahead, and then a brute with a shaven head appeared, cross-armed, to block Hughe's path.

"We asked you *sumthin*," the newcomer rumbled. He flashed a gap-toothed grin.

Hughe halted, looked the brute up and down, and then threw a backward glance over his own shoulder to confirm the first man was closing the distance between them. "My bag is of no concern to you."

"Is that so?" said the smaller of the two men. "See, we disagree."

The knight pulled his cloak back from his hip, exposing his sword, and loosened its scabbard.

"Give us the bag, and maybe we don't spill your guts," said the brute, walking purposefully toward him. A blade glinted in his fist as the moon momentarily came out from behind a cloud.

Hughe slipped his longsword from its scabbard with a metallic rasp.

The shorter, scarred man now brandished a studded wooden cudgel. With his other hand, he stuck two fingers in his mouth and let out a low whistle. In response, there was a thump on the other side of a narrow wooden door on the right side of the alley, followed by the sound of an iron bolt being thrown back. The door opened outward and three scruffy men entered the alley, all bearing curved daggers.

***

Perched above the scene, Dara shook her head again. She recognized the shaven-headed brute. If Kornin was here, then this lot were the Hobblers—vicious cutthroats not even worthy of membership in the Pickers.

Hughe, the foolish… whatever he was, didn't stand a chance against five men, but she wasn't about to get involved in this mess. It was a shame though. He was rather handsome, even if he was a spy.

Dara heard a scuff from the other side of the alley, slightly lower than her position. She looked and saw another man, leaning over a balcony and taking aim at Hughe with a crossbow.

Her lip curled. *Cowards!* Five against one was bad enough but shooting him from the dark was too much. Dara drew a knife from beneath her sleeve and threw it. It spun, point over hilt, whirring across the distance to strike the would-be assassin in the temple with the pommel.

The arbalist and crossbow both tumbled from the balcony and landed in the alley with a heavy thud.

As the echo of the impact faded, everyone's eyes turned upward toward Dara's perch.

She grimaced. *So much for staying out of it.*

***

"Cut him!" the brute shouted, shattering the silence.

They lunged.

Hughe's longsword flashed out, severing the dagger-hand of one latecomer at the wrist.

The man stared wide-eyed as crimson sprayed from the stump, but the other two who had emerged through the narrow door barely seemed to notice. They charged in, stabbing.

Hughe swept his blade in a backhanded arc to knock aside one dagger, then ran the other man through, but the maneuver left him exposed. The scarred thug at his back slammed his cudgel down on the knight's shoulder with a heavy blow.

His teeth ground together but he managed to hold on to his sword. He shot a murderous glance back at the scarred man and then brought his boot down hard, just above the thug's ankle. Bone crunched audibly and the man screamed, crumpling and clutching at his shattered leg.

Hughe pivoted back toward the others just as one slashed at his unprotected middle. He instinctively twisted his upper body.

Instead of gutting him, the dagger slashed his satchel open, spilling the book out into the alley where it tumbled to the grimy cobblestones.

His eyes flashed with anger, and his sword arced downward, shearing through the offender's clavicle.

He yanked at the hilt but before he could free the blade, the shaven-headed brute charged in with his dagger.

The knight caught his attacker's wrist with his free hand and stopped the thrust, but the brute's momentum carried him to the alley wall with a crash. Hughe's sword remained buried in the fallen corpse, just beyond his reach.

The brute outweighed Hughe by a hundred pounds, pressing his bulk into the knight. Hughe's fist was locked around the attacker's knife hand. Tendons stood out in both of their arms as they strained against each other. The brute's other hand found Hughe's throat, tightening in a vicelike grip, and the young knight dug his fingers under it, struggling to pry it loose.

A boot slammed between the brute's legs from behind with a meaty thump, and his grip immediately slacked at Hughe's throat as he simultaneously dropped the knife.

Hughe wasted no time delivering a powerful right hook that sent the brute toppling like a felled tree, revealing the young woman behind him, her boot still poised from the kick.

The knight's eyebrows rose. It was the young woman from the shop.

"I believe the words you're looking for are 'thank you,'" she said.

Hughe recovered quickly, both from the fight and the surprise of seeing her in the alley. "Thank you, sincerely, but what are you doing here...?" He paused, realizing awkwardly that he did not know her name.

"Dara." She gave him a crooked smile. "When I saw you walk into Sinners Alley, I just had to satisfy my curiosity. Do you have a death wish, or are you just stupid?"

He frowned at her and smoothed out his surcoat. "Fair enough, but how did you happen to be nearby? You must have left Tamir's shop only a moment after I did. Coincidence?"

Dara shrugged dismissively and retrieved the dagger she had thrown.

As she slid it back into the sheath beneath her sleeve, Hughe glimpsed the silver inlay on the hilt—a hummingbird in flight, its eyes tiny amethysts that caught the moonlight. It struck him as oddly extravagant for such a plain, practical weapon.

The thug with the missing hand slumped against the wall and slid to the ground. Hughe removed a belt from one of the dead men and tightened it around the amputee's arm, about six inches above the bloody stump.

"Why help him?" Dara scoffed. "This lot would have cut your throat over a loaf of bread."

Hughe picked up the book and wiped it with his cloak. "If it had been a loaf of bread, I would have given it to them. Hold this a moment," he said, handing it to her.

Dara glanced at the tome and then stared at the knight in disbelief. "Why is this damned book so important to you?"

Hughe paused before answering. "We used to have one when I was a boy. An illustrated copy just like this. My mother..."

He let the words trail off before they could betray his emotions and cleared his throat. He could feel Dara studying him as he removed two more belts from the fallen and used them to secure the big brute's wrists behind his back along with his ankles.

"What are you doing that for?" Dara asked.

Hughe looked up at her. "We've got to summon the Watch and tell them what transpired here."

Dara frowned. "Do me a courtesy and leave me out of the tale. Just tell them you vanquished these cutthroats all on your own."

"It would be unbecoming to exaggerate—"

"You're honor bound," Dara said, cutting him off. Her tone brooked no further argument. She handed him back the book.

Hughe nodded. "Go then. I am in your debt. You have my bond, and my thanks. I'll wait until you walk out of sight before I call the Watch."

She scrutinized him with a slight tilt of her head.

Dara gave him a wry smile and scaled the wall with ease.

In seconds, she was atop the roof.

Hughe shook his head as she feigned a curtsy. Then she was gone, vanished into the night.

CHAPTER TWO

The walled, four-story mansion squatted alone on a sprawling corner lot. All its windows were dark, save for a dim glow on the top floor. Even in the creeping dusk, the estate loomed, a world apart from the huddled homes and crooked shops that crowded the neighboring streets.

Just before it turned off the lane, a carriage rattled past the mouth of the alley where a lone priestess in a hooded robe sat cross-legged. An alms bowl was on the ground before her. Prayer beads were draped over her wrists and the holy symbol of the goddess Sibilee dangled from her pressed palms.

The carriage out of sight, the priestess rose languidly, gathering her things.

Dara walked swiftly, and the loose-fitting robes couldn't fully hide the sway of her hips, despite her best efforts. She had lingered all afternoon as close to the Giltwarden's estate as she dared, waiting for him to keep his weekly appointment with the duke.

Dara reached the front corner of the wall that surrounded the estate and headed toward the rear. The tawny-haired thief removed the robe as she walked and cast it aside, revealing a leather bag over one shoulder and a silk cord wrapped in a tight coil around her slim waist. Cradled in the crook of her left arm was a white rabbit with a small brass bell dangling from its neck by a lace collar.

She knelt near the wall. "You'll be fine, little one. You are much faster than them."

Dara gripped a loose stone in the wall and removed it, revealing a hole just big enough for the rabbit.

The thief leaned forward and peered through the hole toward her right. She smelled the heavy musk and sour sweat from the beasts before she saw them.

Dara kissed the rabbit on the head, whispered, "You can do this," and nudged it through the hole.

She immediately peered through the hole again, eager to assure herself of the creature's escape.

The rabbit's nose wriggled feverishly for a moment. Its ears straightened as it registered the pair of slobbering mastiffs approaching.

There was a low growl from both of their throats and then they lunged forward, pulling the armored guard violently along with them. The rabbit turned in the other direction and sprinted as fast as it could, following the perimeter of the wall. The guard dogs swept by Dara's vantage point in a blur, the guard cursing and running with an awkward gait as he tried to keep up.

Dara stood, took several steps back from the wall, and ran toward it, leaping at the last second. Her hands barely reached the top. She swung her legs to one side and then the other like a pendulum, building momentum. With a final swing, she vaulted up and over, lying prone atop the rough, uneven wall for a moment to make sure no other guards were in sight.

She scanned left, then right. This was her best chance.

She rolled off the wall and landed gracefully in a crouch, then sprinted toward the main house, unwinding the silk cord as she ran. It had a tiny iron grappling hook at one end, which she whirled overhead in a tight arc and cast upward.

She tugged the cord to test it, then climbed.

A moment later, the young thief lay flat upon the roof's cool tiles. Gathering up her cord and grappling hook, she crawled toward the front of the mansion and peeked over the edge just in time to see the rabbit dart through the iron gates at the front of the estate. The gate reverberated as the enraged mastiffs slammed into it, slavering and barking at their escaped quarry.

Dara smiled and brought her palm to her lips, blowing a kiss toward her furry co-conspirator. An unnecessary gesture, obviously, but one that felt right to her.

Staying low, she slipped across the tiles toward the back of the estate. Reaching the rear of the mansion, she peered over the roof's edge at the open third-floor balcony below. She hooked her grapple around the weathervane and lowered herself to the balcony with practiced ease.

After looping the silk cord over a sconce in the wall so that it wouldn't be immediately visible to anyone looking out, she tested the door at the back of the balcony. It was unlocked.

Beyond the door was a large bedroom, as expected. The fading light from the balcony revealed a chamber that was lushly decorated with rugs, tapestries, and fine furniture, including a claw-footed bathtub. Of more interest to her was the head of the iron staircase leading down.

An open door led to a hall, but all was quiet.

Dara crept down the first few stairs and into darkness. The thief dared not light a candle because she could not risk the smell giving her away. She had come prepared, however.

Dara removed something from her satchel and freed it from the strips of linen swaddling she had used to protect it. It was a tall glass jar, glowing with winking lights. The wax-sealed parchment lid was pierced with many tiny holes, and inside the jar, dozens of fireflies were flashing rhythmically.

Now able to see, she continued down the spiral stairs, ignoring the second floor, and into a large study on the ground floor where a cherrywood desk sat close by. There was a closed door at the far end of the room, past a pair of high-backed armchairs. Bookcases lined the walls.

Dara made her way purposefully toward one of the bookcases, this one set in an alcove. She ran her fingers under the beveled fronts of the shelves and all around the inside of the frame and smiled with satisfaction when her fingers touched a metal catch.

She was just about to tug on the catch when she heard heavy footfalls approaching the door.

Dara quickly deposited her firefly jar back inside her bag and silently wedged herself between the side of the bookcase and the wall of the alcove. She could not see the door from her hiding place.

She heard the door open, and the flickering light from a candle projected into the room.

The heavy footfalls came closer, and soon a guard wearing a mail hauberk and greaves appeared in the center of the room, just within Dara's field of vision. A sword hung from his belt.

"All is as it should be," the guard said to someone else in the direction of the door.

"Good," came the response. This voice was sibilant. "It is far too close to the feast to have anything upset our plans."

A bald, gaunt figure dressed in a black velvet robe glided into view, stopping before the desk. Dara squeezed herself backward as far as she could. Her heart was beating fast, and she focused on keeping her breath slow and quiet.

The gaunt figure lifted a parchment from the desk and turned toward the door. She could see his profile now. He had a hooked nose and almost skeletal fingers.

Dara had heard rumors of the Giltwarden's strange, cadaver-like seneschal who never left the grounds.

"Double the guard inside the wall," the seneschal hissed.

"It was just a rabbit that got the dogs' blood up," the guard protested.

The corpselike steward stared malevolently at the guard for a dozen heart-beats, silent.

"As you say," the guard relented. He left the room briskly, followed by the seneschal.

Dara heard the door close, and the room was enveloped in darkness once more. She slid out of her hiding place and retrieved the fireflies from her bag.

She quickly located the catch in the bookcase this time and tugged at it. A muffled click sounded from behind the bookcase, and it drifted forward ever so slightly.

Dara grabbed it and pulled it toward her. The bookcase swung into the room like a door.

Cautiously, she held the glowing jar before her, its glow revealing a square, medium-sized chamber beyond.

An odd assortment of items to her right immediately drew her attention. Among more mundane paintings and sculptures, a peculiar book rested on a carved stone plinth beneath a strange painted parchment, crudely nailed to the wall.

The illustration depicted several cross-sections of the human form, with various areas marked in a language foreign to her. Something about it was unsettling—less scholarly and more... forbidden.

Beneath it, the tome was no less unnerving. Its beaten bronze covers were imprinted with strange glyphs. Dara hesitated before opening it. The pages, stitched together with hair, looked like tattooed skin that had been cured. The skin was faded, but the inked images were disturbingly sharp and vibrant. She couldn't make sense of them, but they made her own flesh crawl.

She shuddered and tore her gaze away from the book. At the far end of the chamber, just within the dim glow of her fireflies, a flight of steps descended into darkness. To her left was an iron door with an L-shaped handle and an inset keyhole.

Dara smiled.

The thief set the jar on the floor and saw something that caused her to draw in a sudden, sharp breath. The tile next to the jar was slightly recessed compared to the others surrounding it, and she knew she had narrowly avoided the trigger for something.

She chided her own carelessness as she retrieved the set of lockpicks from under her sleeve and began working on the lock.

A bead of sweat trickled down the back of her neck as she delicately coaxed the tumblers. Finally, she felt them fall into place. Turning the handle, she winced as the door opened with a loud squeal from the hinges.

Dara picked up her fireflies and peered inside. The ten-foot-square vault was brimming with wealth. Chests of gold and silver coins lined the floor of the vault in neat rows and gold trade bars were stacked as high as her knees against the rear wall.

She was pulling a pair of empty canvas sacks from her bag when she heard the faint sound of a woman sobbing.

Dara held perfectly still and listened, straining her ears.

The sobbing came again, this time followed by a woman's voice. "Hush, please. There is no use in it."

The voices were coming from the direction of the stairs at the other end of the hidden room.

Dara stepped out of the vault, avoiding the pressure plate as she retrieved her fireflies. She lingered, conflicted. The coinmaster's hoard was hers for the taking—more wealth than she could ever spend, and no one the wiser. But then her gaze fell again on the unnerving illustration nailed to the wall and the loathsome manuscript beneath it...

She cursed under her breath, and crept toward the stairs.

Having reached them, she took a few tentative steps downward, and called softly, "Hello?"

She held the jar high. What she saw chilled her.

About ten feet below her, at the bottom of the stairs, there was a row of barred cells running along either side of a passage. An iron door loomed at the far end of the corridor.

"What the devil?" Dara whispered.

"Who's there?" called a frantic female voice.

Dara quickly descended the remaining stairs.

A young woman's dirty, tear-streaked face appeared between the bars of the cell closest to the stairs on the right. She had flaxen hair that was unkempt and knotted. Her terror-filled eyes found Dara, and she cried out, "Oh please! Help us!"

The hands and face of a second woman, this one raven-haired and a few years older, appeared at the bars of the opposite cell. "Who are you?" the second woman asked. "Another filthy cannibal?"

"Keep your voices down," Dara cautioned. "No, I'm not a... a cannibal?"

"Yes," the first woman said frantically. "They are disgusting. Let us out!"

"Be quiet," Dara warned again in a hushed whisper. With a wrinkled nose, she added, "The sick bastard."

"Can you let us out of here?" the dark-haired woman asked.

She didn't know these women but leaving them to be eaten wasn't something she could live with. "I'll try," Dara answered.

She brought out her lockpicks again and went to work on the cell holding the frantic younger woman; if she were freed first, it would help keep her silent while she freed her companion. "Is there anyone else down here?" she asked.

"They already ate the others—the ones who were here before they snatched us," the younger, pale-haired woman said. "He laughed when he told us about it."

After a moment, Dara had the door open, and the young woman leaped from the cell. Dara caught her by the wrist. "Wait," she said. "You'll bring a half dozen guards down on our heads if you go running out of here like you've got the devil chasing you."

The girl nodded uncertainly, and Dara added, in a compassionate tone, "We'll all leave together as soon as I get her free."

She worked as quickly as she could on the lock of the second cell and soon had it open. "Stay behind me and don't make a sound."

The pair followed her quietly enough up the stairs and they reached the hidden room.

They were almost to the other side when the younger woman lurched past Dara to get through the door. She stepped on the pressure plate as she pushed past, and it sunk two inches into the surrounding floor with an audible click.

Clarion bells rang deafeningly from somewhere within the mansion.

Dara cursed. "We have to go. Quickly! Just follow me and don't stray again."

She ran toward the spiral staircase that would lead them to the upper floors, but heavy footfalls above changed Dara's mind.

"Change of plan," she blurted, and led them to the door across the room. From her study of the schematics, she knew there was a parlor on the other side of this door, and beyond the parlor... the main entrance. Not the safest exit, but certainly the most direct.

Dara threw open the door, and they rushed across the parlor, past two large settees. As they reached the other side of the parlor and entered a foyer, a flickering light appeared at the front door. It was the bald seneschal, holding an oil lamp.

The trio lurched to a stop.

Dara unsheathed her dagger and growled, "Step aside."

The seneschal sneered. "As you wish." He stepped to the left, but as he did so, he seemed to blur and divide into two identical figures, leaving one in front of the exit. Then that figure stepped to the right and divided again.

Three identical grinning seneschals now stood in their way, their oil lamps swaying in their hands.

Heavy footfalls and the jangle of armor preceded four guards as they ran through the parlor and into the foyer. Two guards grabbed the struggling dark-haired woman and the screaming younger one.

The other two came after Dara. She kicked one in the groin and slashed the other across the face with her dagger.

A shock like electricity struck Dara's wrist and her dagger flew from her hand to clatter across the floor of the foyer and into the parlor, where it came to rest under one of the settees.

She turned toward her attacker, one of the three seneschals who had touched her with his bare hand. Quick as a serpent, another stepped forward, his hand flicking toward her and touching her softly in the center of her forehead. Pain lanced through her skull.

She was unconscious before she struck the floor.

CHAPTER THREE

Hughe had nearly completed his inventory report of the barrack's larder when a timid knock at his door halted the scratching of his quill.

The knight looked up from the desk in his small but tidy chamber. "Come in," he invited.

The door opened, and Peter, the fourteen-year-old beanpole of a squire who had been assigned to him, stuck his eager face and mop of unruly, straw-colored hair into the chamber. He came from lesser, rural nobility like Hughe himself, and the knight rather liked the lad.

"What is it, Peter?"

"Sir, there is a man asking for you at the gate. He says his name is Tamir."

Hughe felt a twinge of unease upon hearing the name. He had no idea what could have prompted this visit from the shop owner, but he was already in enough jeopardy over the incident in the alley.

"I'll be right there," he answered, finally.

The boy retreated from the chamber as the knight stood.

"Peter?" Hughe called him back.

The boy's face quickly reappeared. "Yes, sir?"

"Just call me Hughe, unless the situation dictates formality. We've talked about this already."

Peter nodded, then hurried away.

Leaving his room behind, Hughe shut the door and walked to the arch at the center of a U-shaped corridor. As of last week, this was his home, at least temporarily, the barracks where he and other knights fulfilling their obligation to the duke were garrisoned.

Thiardun was Gauldün's easternmost city and its last true bastion of civilization, aside from a few baronial border holdings like his father's. It required a ready military force should the scattered rival tribes of Besh beyond it ever choose to unify. Though Gauldün had clashed with their chieftains many times over the generations, they hadn't posed a serious threat since the fall of the Beshan king, before Hughe's birth.

In his decade as both knight and squire, he'd fought far more outlaws and bandits than Beshan warriors.

Hughe turned, passed through the arch, and strode through the great hall where the men gathered for meals. Exiting the hall, he crossed the yard and arrived at the barracks gate, where Peter had returned to his post, alongside another squire.

Just outside the open, iron gate stood Tamir, his face lined with worry. Relief softened his features when he spotted Hughe.

The knight did his best to put on a pleasant expression. "This is an unexpected visit. What can I do for you, Tamir?"

"Can we talk privately?" the shop owner asked.

Hughe glanced toward the sun. "Unfortunately, I have an appointment with the commander."

"It really is important, and it will only take a moment." The older man's tone was almost desperate.

Hughe gave him a terse nod. "All right, but I really do have just a moment." He joined Tamir outside the gate.

Tamir made a gesture indicating the knight should follow him, and the pair began to walk the perimeter.

Hughe held his tongue. He could feel his impatience rising, but it was obvious the shopkeeper wanted to get beyond earshot of the gate.

They turned the corner and took a few more paces.

"It is Dara," the older man said in a rush. "She is missing. I fear she may have been kidnapped, or worse, and I need you to accompany me to the Giltwarden's estate."

Hughe halted abruptly and turned to the older man. "Why do you think she's been kidnapped? And..." he added in a harsh whisper, "what do you want with the coinmaster?"

Tamir sighed and looked down at his feet. "I think she may have gone to his mansion to rob him."

"*What?*" Hughe blurted. "Why would you think that?"

Tamir looked up into the knight's incredulous face and locked eyes with him. "All right. I know she went there to rob him. She told me as much. But that was two nights ago, and I have not seen or heard from her since. It is not like her. Not with me, anyway. Something must have happened to her."

Hughe could feel his pulse throbbing in his neck. "Just knowing this and doing nothing to stop it is enough to be considered an accomplice." He crossed his arms. "You should be looking for her in the Iron Roost, not at the coinmaster's home."

"I have been to the tower already!" Tamir all but shouted. "They do not have her."

Hughe blanched. "You did what?"

"Well of course I did not mention anything about the Giltwarden or a plot to rob him. I am no fool!"

After his outburst, Tamir's expression softened. "I know something happened to her at the mansion. If she is still alive, she is there. I just need to speak with the coinmaster, and I need you to accompany me."

"You can't just go to the Giltwarden and make wild accusations—"

Tamir held his hand up. "We will say that I came to you with information about a plot to rob him and that you insisted we go and warn him immediately. I will not mention Dara specifically, but if he knows anything, I will be able to prove it to you."

Hughe looked doubtful.

The older man continued. "I know a spell. A minor... geas."

"Sorcery?" Hughe's brow furrowed, lips parted in disbelief.

"It is not so uncommon in Mar-Üd, my homeland," Tamir protested. "Once we are face-to-face, I will discreetly enchant the coinmaster. I cannot compel him to tell the truth, but the glamour will render him unable to tell us a lie."

The knight shook his head. "I don't know."

The shopkeeper pressed on. "Once we confirm he has Dara, I will turn myself in to the constable if I must. I will tell him everything. I would rather she face legitimate justice beside me than in some secret dungeon at the hands of a depraved noble."

"My conduct here is already under scrutiny."

Tamir's voice sharpened. "As I understand it, you owe Dara a debt. If not for her, you would be rotting in Sinners Alley!"

The knight took a step back before meeting the shopkeeper's furious stare.

The older man's voice broke as he continued with barely controlled emotion. "She was only six years old when I rescued her from a slaver's block in Besh. She has been with me ever since. She is like a daughter to me. I just need your help to get an audience with the Giltwarden. Nothing more. No matter what happens after that, you can hold to the original story... that I approached you with information and you were ensuring that he received the warning."

Hughe shifted uneasily. He knew he shouldn't be involved in a deception against the coinmaster... or anyone else for that matter. Especially now. But Dara *had* saved his life.

"I'll accompany you," he said finally. "See that you get an audience. Take part in your charade about warning him of an impending robbery. But that is all. If you choose to go to the constable after that, you must tell them that you deceived me as well."

Tamir gave the knight a small, hopeful smile. "I swear it."

"I must keep my appointment with the commander first and learn if I am to be punished for recent events," Hughe said. "Sunset is about an hour from now. If I'm not already in irons by then, I will meet you at your shop."

Tamir touched the knight's arm, a look of gratitude on his face.

Hughe watched the shopkeeper walk away and disappear among the thinning crowd across the street, where merchants were packing away their goods and closing up their stalls in preparation for the approaching evening. The smells of fresh bread and smoked sweetmeats still lingered in the air.

He turned to head back to the gate—and froze.

There it was again... the faint scuff of leather on stone.

And another. Fainter. Receding.

His fingers found his hilt as a shadow slipped past the wall's edge.

Hughe moved fast, sword half-drawn. As he rounded the wall, he came face-to-face with the eavesdropper.

CHAPTER FOUR

"I think she is waking up," said a young woman's voice.

Dara's first sensation upon returning to consciousness was the feeling of the cold, damp stone beneath her back. Her head throbbed and her eyes ached in their sockets. She opened them slowly. It was pitch black. Her mouth and throat were completely parched.

"Where am I?" She sat up, nausea spinning through her skull.

"You're in hell just like us," the female answered.

The sick feeling passed. Her fingers brushed cold iron bars.

The memory of the secret room inside the coinmaster's home came flooding back.

Dara checked for her lockpicks, but they were gone. So was her dagger. "Damn it." She was quiet for a moment. "All right. We need to make a plan. My name is Dara. What are yours?"

"Nora. Not that it matters. That's Avetta."

Dara recognized the woman who was speaking, Nora, as the dark-haired and more collected of the two women she had broken out of their cells.

"How long have I been unconscious?" she asked.

"Who knows," said a younger, more frightened-sounding voice—Avetta, the pale-haired one. "He's brought us bread a few times since putting us back in our cells. At least one day. Maybe two."

"Who?" Dara asked. "That walking corpse?"

"No," answered Nora. "That is Talbot. He commands the others, but he rarely comes down here. No, she means the giant. Their butcher. He is the one who brings the bread and taunts us with what they plan to do."

"Wait." Dara was confused. "That sorcerer, Talbot, is the coinmaster's seneschal. But where is the Giltwarden? Does he know we are prisoners inside his home?"

"I don't know anything about the Giltwarden," Nora responded. "But Talbot is the one who tells the others what to do."

"Well, Nora. Avetta. We are getting out of here. First, I need water."

"Feel around near the bars," Avetta said. "There is a little stone trough there."

Dara explored the floor near the bars tentatively with her fingers until she found a shallow trough full of liquid, just as the girl had promised. The thief leaned down and sniffed. It was musty, but not enough to stop her.

She dribbled a few drops onto her parched tongue. It wasn't wine, but it seemed safe enough. Dara lapped at the trough until it was empty.

Her thirst sated, Dara stood carefully. "There must be something in here I can use to get this door open. Can you tell me how you came to be here while I look?"

Avetta answered first, her voice subdued. "I was on Weavers Row. My ma sent me to buy thread. She told me not to talk to strangers, but on the way back, there was a tart vendor. I wanted to buy one for my little brother, and then he offered me another for free, and…" Her voice trailed off.

Nora continued the tale. "She woke up here. It was almost the same for me. I was at the Dancing Pig, and a smooth-talking bastard bought me some wine. I should have known better," she added bitterly. "But by the time I realized something was wrong with the drink and stumbled out into the alley, there were rough hands waiting to grab me."

Dara said nothing. She couldn't see their faces in the dark, but their voices told her enough. Her jaw tightened.

There was a squeal of hinges from above, and a dim light reached into the gloom.

A steady glow descended toward them, accompanied by lightly treading footsteps.

The cadaverous seneschal soon stood between their cells, holding an oil lamp, with another man on his left.

It was Lord Corgrith, the Giltwarden. He looked ill. The coinmaster was well past middle-aged, and had always been slender, but now he looked emaciated, like his seneschal.

Corgrith's eyes were bright and alert, but his salt-and-pepper hair seemed to be falling out.

"So, you are finally awake," Talbot said to Dara. "That is good. I would hate for you to sleep away your final hours. Especially on this auspicious occasion. Tonight, we hold a feast in a sacred place, and we will honor our guests with your flesh."

Dara bared her teeth and growled, "Touch us again, and I swear I'll see you dead."

Talbot casually waved his hand and chuckled. "Defiant girl. I can render you senseless just as easily as I did before, but it would be a shame. You see, fear makes the meat sweeter, and you will soon be very afraid."

Corgrith laughed softly. "Pretty eyes," he said, a string of drool stretching from his lips as he reached a frail, trembling hand toward Avetta. He was interrupted by a fit of coughing that rattled in his chest.

The seneschal pulled a brass ring on the wall near the stairs and a bell gonged from somewhere beyond the cells.

With a thundering clang, the iron door at the end of the corridor flew open.

Heavy footsteps heralded something large.

When the newcomer was revealed in the lamplight, all Dara's bravado fled from her. Her face betrayed the horror she felt at the sight of him.

The man who now stood between their cells, towering over Talbot and Corgrith, was a hulking pillar of brutality. He was extraordinarily tall, wearing darkly stained leathers, with furs draped over his muscular frame. His tunic was sleeveless, exposing hairy bulging arms, and his face and hands were deeply scarred. His hair was long and greasy, and his nose appeared to have been broken multiple times.

The massive newcomer took a ring full of keys from his belt and fitted one into the lock of Dara's cell. She stepped backward as he entered until she reached the rear wall. Then, cornered, she sprang at him, leaping forward and snapping her foot into his groin.

Unfazed, the brute responded with a backhanded slap that sent Dara crashing into the wall where she slumped to the floor.

Talbot gave a dry laugh. "You'll find Cullyn much less... sensitive... than other men."

CHAPTER FIVE

The surprise was evident on Tamir's face when he hastily opened the door to his shop and found the tall boy with straw-colored hair standing next to Hughe on the stoop.

"This is my squire, Peter. He is coming with us, but only because I caught him eavesdropping on our conversation earlier."

"Hughe," the boy protested, "I swear I only came to tell you the commander was ready to see you. I didn't mean to spy. By the time I realized it was a private conversation, it was too late."

Hughe cast a sidelong glance at his squire. "This is one of those situations that calls for more formality."

"Yes, sir," the boy said with downcast eyes.

"In any event," Hughe continued, "the boy is coming with us."

"It matters not to me, as long as we waste no more time." Tamir grabbed a satchel from a hook near the door and placed the strap around his neck.

The trio made their way quickly through the streets.

The moon was just beginning to rise when they arrived at the gate of the Giltwarden's estate. They were announced by the deep baying and growling of dogs, out of sight on the other side of the wall.

Through the gate and across the courtyard, they saw the mansion's entrance, lit only by oil lamps flanking the great door. The rest of the property lay in darkness.

A pair of leashed mastiffs and their handlers, two grim-looking men in hauberks, appeared on the other side of the gate in short order. Each wore a longsword.

"What do you want?" the first guard, a thick man with dusky skin, asked curtly.

Tamir looked at Hughe expectantly.

The knight cleared his throat. "We need to speak to the coinmaster. It is very urgent."

"He isn't in," barked the second guard, who was taller and leaner than the first.

"I see," said Hughe.

"Can we await his return inside?" Tamir offered. "It really is a matter of extreme importance."

"He won't be back until tomorrow," countered the first guard.

Hughe turned toward Tamir with his palms turned out in a gesture of futility.

Undeterred, Tamir pressed. "If we could just speak with his seneschal then. We have information regarding a threat against this house, and it is our duty to report it."

"You can report it to us." The guard's expression was stone.

"I mean you no offense, young man," Tamir said, "but what if you yourself are implicated in this plot?"

Hughe jumped in. "Perhaps it would be best to summon the constable and bring him here, since the heads of the house are unavailable."

The guards exchanged a dark look.

"Wait here." The taller guard pulled his mastiff toward the mansion, leaving the others behind in tense silence, broken only by the snarling of the second dog.

By the time he returned, the moon had fully risen. "The seneschal will see you inside."

They unlocked the gate and escorted the visitors across the courtyard, struggling to restrain their barking dogs. With a grunt, the taller one passed his leash to the other guard and dragged the heavy door wide, jerking his head to indicate they should enter.

"Have a seat. Wait for him there, and do not wander."

Tamir entered first, with Hughe close and Peter bringing up the rear. As the squire crossed the threshold, the door slammed shut behind him.

They stood in a darkened entryway, but the chamber beyond was brightly lit.

Leaving the foyer, they stepped into a well-appointed parlor. A freshly lit fire blazed in the hearth on the left-hand side of the room. Two large settees faced each other in the center, and at the far end, opposite the foyer, a tall mirror stood on an iron stand beside a closed door. Several oil lamps hung in reflective sconces along the walls, and a copper brazier between the settees exuded a cloying scent that filled the parlor.

Tamir and Peter sat on the nearer settee, leaving the other to Hughe, with the mirror at its back.

Something about the mirror unsettled the knight, and he studied it briefly.

It was taller than he was, its frame carved from petrified oak. The glass was dim despite the well-lit room, and he had the oddest feeling its dullness came not from tarnish—but from it being a window into another, darker place.

Hughe shook his head and quietly scoffed at himself, then took a seat with his back to it.

Tamir's eyes lingered on the mirror behind Hughe before his gaze met the knight's. "You must admit the guards' behavior is strange."

Hughe glanced over his shoulder to ensure they were still alone.

The mirror caught his eye again, and he had the distinct feeling it was watching them somehow. Listening.

He turned back to Tamir and the squire. "I don't disagree, but we are playing at a dangerous game. If you're wrong—"

"*Wrong* about what?" a voice, tinted with mockery, asked from behind him.

Tamir, Hughe, and Peter all got quickly to their feet. Hughe turned to face the newcomer. Their black-robed host was tall and thin, his bald head and hooked nose giving him a vulturelike appearance. His eye sockets were sunken and ringed with shadows, but within those hollowed cavities, the eyes themselves were sharp and knowing.

Hughe was surprised he had not heard the man approach. The door was still closed and neither Tamir nor Peter had shown any indication they had seen the man enter the room.

It was Tamir who recovered first. "My name is Tamir. My companions are Sir Hughe and his squire. Are you the Giltwarden's seneschal?"

"I am, but you have not answered my question." The steward sneered. "What might you be wrong about?"

"We came seeking an audience with the Giltwarden. We bring warning of a plot to rob him. Sir Hughe was only worrying over the impropriety of disturbing your house so late in the evening, especially should it prove to be false." Tamir gave Hughe a subtle nod.

"How interesting," the seneschal replied.

Tamir didn't respond. The silence stretched between them, making Hughe's nerves grow tauter with every passing second.

Hughe looked at the shopkeeper, whose lips moved slightly as he muttered an incantation under his breath, his gaze fixed on the seneschal.

Wanting to buy Tamir a moment to finish the enchantment, as inconceivable as it seemed to him, Hughe continued with the ruse. "We have reason to believe the thieves have somehow acquired knowledge of a secret vault here in the mansion."

The seneschal laughed humorlessly. "I assure you," he replied with a thick sibilance, "the coinmaster has no such vault on the grounds. Only a small strongbox, the location of which I will not disclose. I am sure you understand."

"There was a young woman who brought us this information," Tamir spoke suddenly, in a commanding voice, his eyes locking with their host. "She may have come to warn the Giltwarden on her own. Auburn hair. Green eyes. Have you seen her?"

A contemptuous look came over the seneschal's face. "No such person has been here. Neither the Giltwarden nor I have received a warning from anyone. Now, if there is nothing else, I must return to my duties."

The shopkeeper's jaw tensed, uncertainty in his eyes.

Hughe gave Tamir a stern glance. "We should go."

"Are you sure a young woman has not been here?" Tamir stepped around the settee and began to advance toward the seneschal. "Her name is Dara." Perspiration beaded on his brow. His expression was still earnest, but his confidence had abandoned him.

The look of contempt faded from the seneschal's wan face. His countenance became predatory, his eyes boring into the shopkeeper, bringing him to a halt. "I do hope I will not need to summon the guards."

"Come. We are leaving," Hughe said to Tamir, his tone stern.

Tamir's expression hardened, and he drew himself up. "I am not leaving until I see the vault." His voice rose, cracking with strain. "I know you have Dara!"

Hughe stared, the certainty in the old man's voice sounding less sure and more desperate. He could feel the situation spinning out of control. Why had he been so reckless to allow the shopkeeper to convince him to come along?

Tamir advanced toward the seneschal once more.

The steward took a step back. "Guards!" he called. The summons was immediately followed by the sound of jangling mail and heavy footfalls.

Peter crouched to retrieve something glinting from the shadows and dust beneath the settee.

"Let's go!" Hughe took Tamir firmly by the upper arm.

Peter rose quickly, turning the object over in his hands.

Both the knight and the shopkeeper ignored the boy as the former attempted to redirect the latter away from the seneschal.

Three guards appeared then, hands on the pommels of their swords.

"Damn it!" Hughe was losing his patience with the older man squirming in his grasp.

Tamir suddenly stiffened, his eyes locked on what Peter held.

Hughe turned.

It was a dagger with a silver hummingbird inlaid in the hilt, its eyes twin specks of amethyst.

Dara's dagger.

Hughe's brow narrowed. She *had* been here.

CHAPTER SIX

Hughe's scowl deepened. He pictured the struggle that must have sent the dagger beneath the settee, where it had been missed by the oafish guards.

He released the shopkeeper and drew his longsword with a hiss of steel. The guards responded in kind, their swords scraping free from their scabbards.

"It seems you have not been honest with us, sir," the knight said with a scowl. "Now tell us where the girl is."

Several things happened at once. Tamir lunged toward the seneschal. One of the guards slashed his sword at the shopkeeper, but Hughe was faster, blocking the strike with his own.

Amid the clash of steel, Peter cursed as he grabbed the copper brazier, searing his palms. Grimacing, he threw it into the faces of the other two guards who were just rounding the settee.

Tamir, heedless of the near-fatal blow or the knight's intervention, grabbed the seneschal by the front of his robe. The steward's frame shimmered for an instant then simply wasn't there. The old man looked at his empty hands in astonishment.

Hughe gave the high back of the settee a solid kick, sending it crashing into his foe's legs and knocking him prone. As the fallen guard struggled to rise, the knight drove his sword into the back of his neck.

Peter stood transfixed, eyes wide, as blood pooled beneath the fallen man.

The other two guards finished swatting at the hot coals from the brazier. The smell of their burnt hair vied with the heavy, sweet smell that had been present before. Both had newly forming blisters on their faces. Enraged, they charged after the squire, and Peter, his face pale, dashed behind the other settee that was still upright.

Hughe pivoted and slashed, laying one of the rushing guards open from hip to shoulder as Peter shielded his eyes with his arm.

The remaining guard turned to face the knight.

The two squared off briefly before lunging. Blades whistled through the air. Steel rang through the chamber as their swords collided and parted. Once. Twice. A third savage clash.

There was a crunch as the links of the guard's hauberk snapped apart and a foot of steel sprang from between his shoulders.

Hughe braced his free hand against the guard's chest and, ignoring the man's death grimace, jerked his sword free.

He turned to the shopkeeper. "Where the hell did he go?"

"He was never here!" Tamir snapped. "That is why the spell did not work. Quickly, I know where the vault is!"

"Wait!" Peter dashed to the foyer door, bolted it, and ran back. "That'll keep the dogs out for a moment!" he shouted, between rapid breaths.

Seeing Tamir vanish through the doorway, Hughe and Peter dashed past the mirror and into an adjoining study, where the shopkeeper was examining a bookcase set within an alcove.

The old man ran his hands along the inside of the bookcase until there was a click and then the case swung outward from the wall.

Realizing it was on a hinge, Hughe pulled it fully open, exposing a dark, rectangular opening.

Peter grabbed an oil lamp from the elaborate desk on the other side of the room and lit it before handing it to Hughe.

The lamp revealed an iron door on the left, a stairwell descending ahead, and to the right, a display of paintings and sculptures. But as Tamir started to turn away from the art, something else caught his eye, arresting him mid-step.

"Millenoth," Hughe swore, his blood chilling as he gazed upon an esoteric diagram of a human body. The language was foreign, yet it still conveyed a dark purpose.

Tamir was focused on something else, however, a bronze-bound tome resting on a carved piece of stone beneath the diagram. "This cannot be," the scribe said, barely audible. He opened the book and slowly scanned the first page.

"What is it?" the knight asked, frowning.

Tamir's mouth worked silently, and a stunned look spread across his face.

Hughe grabbed the book to get the old shop owner's attention but recoiled when his fingers touched the pages. They were slick and strangely warm. "What is this book, man? Speak!"

"It bears the mark of Ghazir Gal-Uth," Tamir said, wide-eyed. "The author of the *Legamathan*."

"The what?" Hughe asked, exasperated. "I've no idea what you are talking about."

Tamir's gaze hardened. "Something I had believed was only a myth. Ghazir was said to have been a scholar who descended into necromancy, gathering his revelations into a single codex, known as the *Legamathan*. This volume appears to have been his grimoire—or perhaps one of many. A precursor to the darkness that followed. I do not know what dark plot we have begun to uncover here, but we must find Dara. Now!"

Hughe turned and tried the L-shaped handle on the iron door behind them, opposite the art and foul manuscript, but it was locked.

They rushed to the far end of the room and descended the stairs, which landed at one end of a corridor with barred cells running the length of it on either side. There was another iron door at the far end.

Peter's stunned expression mirrored Hughe's own. "How could a respected lord have something like this hidden beneath his home?" he asked in a hushed voice.

Tamir was frantic. "I knew it would be something like this!" He hurried past the cells and found them all to be empty. "Where is she?"

The shopkeeper opened the metal door just as Hughe and Peter joined him. They were greeted by a foul, rotten smell. On their left, an opening revealed a small room with a sleeping pallet and an unlit brazier within.

It was the larger chamber directly ahead that both sickened and chilled them.

In the center of the chamber was a wooden worktable big enough for a person to lie upon. Its surface was scoured with numerous cuts, and it was stained a deep red. A manacle secured by a chain hung from each corner. Several wickedly sharp knives and cleavers hung from hooks in the ceiling over the table. The floor was also stained red and there was a drain there covered by an iron grill.

Hughe's stomach turned. Peter swallowed, eyes darting around the chamber.

Tamir choked back a sob, visibly shaken. His hands hung limply at his sides.

The knight surveyed the rest of the room. On the other side, a rack held several spears. A belted sword hung around one of the leaning shafts. Next to the rack was an open crate.

Hughe looked inside the crate. It contained a jumble of torches. Taking one up, he used the oil lamp to light it.

"I found something!" Peter called, now at the far end of the room. "There is a draft here. I think it is a door." His discovery seemed to have returned some of the color to his face.

Tamir rushed to Peter's side.

Hughe joined his squire and the scribe. He handed the oil lamp to Tamir. After a quick examination of the wall, they found no hidden catch or lever.

The knight began to push against the door and Peter followed suit. Slowly the slab of stone began to move, grinding open inch by inch.

When it would move no further, there was a wide gap at either side.

Tamir hurried past them, through the gap. Hughe returned to the crate and removed two more torches. Then he took a spear from the rack and handed it to the boy, along with one of the unlit torches, before taking another spear for himself.

Tamir reappeared at the far end of the room with a wild, desperate look on his face. Seeing his companions had armed themselves with spears, he strode toward them and took the sword belt from the rack. He drew the sword, and his knuckles were white when he returned it to the scabbard and secured the belt around his waist. Without another word he turned toward the hidden door with Hughe and Peter right behind.

CHAPTER SEVEN

Ankles bound with rope and wrists tied behind her back, Dara lay on her side on the cold stone. The butcher had roughly dropped her there a few moments ago; something had alarmed the seneschal and brought the grim procession to a halt.

Along with Talbot and his gruesome henchman, the coinmaster and three of his guards accompanied them on their subterranean journey. The guards all carried torches.

Nora and Avetta, their hands also bound behind their backs, were tethered to ropes around their necks controlled by two of the guards.

The seneschal cursed and looked up from the tiny mirror in his hand. "There are two men and a boy looking for that one." He pointed at Dara. Scoffing lightly, he added, "No matter. If they happen to find their way into these depths, they will certainly lose their way and starve to death... if they aren't eaten by something else first."

Now that she was no longer hanging over the hulking brute's shoulder, Dara's head began to clear, and she started to make out the details of their surroundings.

They were near the center of a vast intersection. The ground beneath them was paved with cobblestone, which she found odd since they were so far underground. Around the perimeter of the circular chamber, numerous arches pierced the curved walls.

"Come," Talbot said.

The monstrous brute hoisted Dara effortlessly from the ground, threw her over his shoulder once more, and the procession resumed.

The seneschal led them through one of the arches.

CHAPTER EIGHT

Worry for his adopted daughter warped Tamir's sense of time as they descended deeper beneath the city.

It felt like they had been walking the broad subterranean passage for days. But the second of their three torches still burned, proof it had only been an hour or two.

The corridor ended unexpectedly and opened into a broad, circular chamber festooned with many arches.

"How will we know which way to go?" Peter asked, looking around in wonder.

Tamir circled the chamber, eyes scanning the arches, fists clenching at his sides.

Exhaling slowly, he knelt and retrieved a papyrus scroll from his bag, along with a clay pot. Tearing a strip from his robe, he soaked it with oil from the pot before touching his torch to it. As it burned, he read from the papyrus in a strange language. Then he removed another small object from his bag.

It was a cloth doll.

Hughe and his squire exchanged a questioning look.

"This was hers," Tamir said softly. "She carried it everywhere when she was a young girl. I kept it, like a sentimental old fool."

He set the doll on the burning cloth and soon it too was alight. The shopkeeper began to read from the scroll once more before placing it among the flames, which quickly consumed it along with the doll.

"*Dak Su Mata,*" Tamir intoned, staring intently into the small fire. "Show me where."

Smoke coalesced above the ashes, taking on a crude, shifting humanoid outline. The figure floated higher, pausing several feet above the fire before drifting slowly across the chamber.

Tamir gave his astonished companions a weary look. "I will not be able to do that again."

The smoke figure reached the arch and dissipated as if it had encountered a sudden gust.

Without another word, they followed where the smoke had led and passed beneath the same arch.

CHAPTER NINE

After a vertigo-inducing descent down the precariously twisting stairs, Dara was thrown onto the hard, stone floor.

Still bound by her restraints, she lay near the end of a wooden table. Rolling to her other side, she found herself near the base of a monstrous idol with a bestial face, swollen breasts, and many arms.

Nora and Avetta sat between her and the idol, shivering. The ropes around their necks had been tied together.

Dara told herself not to panic. Panic would blind her, and she could not afford to miss her moment when it came.

She rolled back toward the table so that she could see their captors.

Two of the guards placed candles around the table and lit them. At the far end, Talbot fastidiously arranged an array of objects that mirrored those held by the idol. The coinmaster sat to his left.

The seneschal pointed at Nora. "Let's start with that one."

The dark-haired woman tried to pull away from the butcher, but it was useless. He sliced the tether with a large knife and hefted her from the ground with one hand. She screamed as he dropped her on the table and her head smacked against the wood.

"Why not start with me, coward?" Dara shouted. She struggled into a kneeling position where she could reach the ropes around her ankles.

"Do not fret," Talbot mocked. "Your turn will come sooner than you imagine. Others are coming to join our feast, here before the visage of Yam-Eshdu."

The hulking butcher raised the knife above Nora, and she screamed.

"No," Talbot said. He raised a hand before the butcher's knife could fall.

The tendons in the butcher's neck creaked as he turned toward the seneschal.

"Thank you," Nora whimpered, mistaking Talbot's interruption for mercy.

"Let our patron prepare the first for our guests," he said with a sly smile.

The butcher extended the knife to the coinmaster, who reached for it with a shaky hand.

Nora screamed again, thrashing wildly.

"Don't!" Dara bellowed. She almost had the knot at her wrists undone.

Corgrith plunged the knife into Nora's breast. She inhaled sharply and let out a single sob that transformed into a wet gurgle. Slowly she grew still and quiet.

Dara closed her eyes in disgust. When she opened them again, the coinmaster was feebly attempting to pull the knife free from the dead woman's body.

Her jaw clenched. Whatever else transpired here, she would see the bastards dead.

"Lord Corgrith requires your assistance," the seneschal said to the butcher, who eagerly took the knife back from the coinmaster.

An otherworldly glow radiated from a passage to Dara's right, beyond the idol and opposite the stair.

Dara became aware of a presence nearby, as did Talbot and the others.

"They are here," he whispered.

Backlit by the eerily diffused luminescence, three hunched, naked forms appeared. She could not make out many details about the newcomers, other than the yellow glint in their eyes that reflected the candlelight from the table. They reeked of grave spices and putrescence.

Avetta began to shudder uncontrollably.

Talbot beckoned the creatures. "Come and join us. We have just begun to prepare this one for you."

The creatures stood their ground warily. Their heads moved up and down as they made quiet yipping noises to each other.

"Perhaps you prefer one of the others? Take your pick. We intend to share them all. We only ask *you* to share the secret that shields you from the ravages of time."

The creature closest to Dara turned slowly toward her and Avetta. It took a step forward, snuffling at the air. Its skin was a sickly gray. A red blemish covered most of its brow. It had no nose, only a boney ridge with tiny nostril slits.

It took another step. A string of rancid saliva stretched from the corner of its misshapen mouth. Filthy claws curled at the ends of its long, dirt-stained fingers.

Something whistled over Dara's head.

The ghoul lurched backward as the wooden haft of a spear appeared in its chest.

Hughe charged from the darkness, drawing his sword to replace the spear he had thrown. Tamir and Peter were right beside him, the old man waving a sword overhead like a madman and the boy brandishing a spear.

Chaos erupted as the guards drew swords, bracing for the attack.

The ring and clash of steel followed, echoing through the gallery.

One of the guards fell before Hughe's onslaught, throat slashed, and he risked a sweeping glance around the vast space.

The other two guards pressed Peter, but the boy kept them at bay with his spear's superior reach. Tamir rushed past, around the table, clearly intent on Talbot.

Hughe looked toward Dara and saw that her hands were free. She rolled nimbly toward the sword dropped by the slain guard and snatched it up. She used it to make quick work of the rope around her ankles before rushing back to free the other girl.

His concern for his companions nearly cost Hughe his head then, but he managed to interpose his sword between his neck and the axe whooshing toward it at the last instant. Even so, the impact nearly jarred the weapon from his grip.

A grotesque ogre of a man stood before him. Hughe's insides tightened as he appraised his enemy. Every aspect of the giant promised him a gory death.

The knight shook off the fear grasping him and squared off with the butcher.

As Hughe and his monstrous foe circled each other, he caught another glimpse of Tamir. The shopkeeper drew back his sword, but before he could strike Talbot down, the seneschal blew something from his hand toward the scribe. A cloud of vapor enveloped them both, thinning quickly to reveal three identical Talbots encircling Tamir.

His focus snapped back to his own peril as the giant advanced, savagely beating his axe against Hughe's sword with the fury of a smith at his forge. It took all the knight's strength to block and parry as he was driven backward, but at every opportunity he struck back with grim precision.

He was panting for air when he found the edge of the table against the back of his legs. The butcher bled from several places on his arms and torso, but his face was a mask of rage, and he appeared oblivious to his wounds.

The butcher pressed the head of his axe toward Hughe's face while the knight strained to keep it at bay, gripping his sword with both hands. Through slitted eyes he saw one of the two guards harrying Peter pulled to the ground by a snapping ghoul.

A feeble scream got the butcher's attention then, and they both turned their heads to see another ghoul dragging the coinmaster toward the ominous green light.

Hughe took advantage of the giant's distraction. Shifting his weight, he wrenched his sword free of the axe and drove it up under the butcher's muscled arm, piercing his ribcage and heart.

The giant toppled forward, his bulk crushing Hughe against the edge of the table.

Dara cut Avetta free, then turned and froze.

Tamir faced three identical Talbots, circling him like vultures. She watched in horror as one of them darted forward and touched the old man's elbow. Tamir cried out and his sword slipped from his fingers, clattering to the ground.

Without hesitation, she ran to the aid of her mentor, leaving the trembling Avetta behind.

All three Talbots had their daggers poised to strike.

Dara sprinted toward them, knowing she could not block all three blades. At the last moment, she dropped into a forward roll and rose on one knee between her mentor and the seneschal's copies, hoping that if she chose wrong, she would take the blow meant for Tamir.

Her blade rang against steel—her instincts had been true. She batted the dagger away and thrust her sword into Talbot's lower abdomen. The two false Talbots shimmered and disappeared.

That was when she saw Avetta bolt toward the receding green glow, panic overtaking her again.

"Avetta, no!" she shouted, and sprinted after her.

Hughe saw Dara run after the girl, heading toward the strange emerald light.

The knight shoved the dead giant to the floor and raced after Dara just as she disappeared into the glowing tunnel. Tamir and Peter grabbed candles from the table, averting their gaze from the dead woman, and hurried after him.

The glow faded just before they turned a corner, and they skidded to a halt before running headlong into a dead end, their footfalls still echoing in the tunnel.

There was no sign of Dara or the girl.

"I don't understand." Hughe whirled left, then right, in obvious confusion. "They were right here!" He slammed his fist into the solid wall.

Tamir held his candle high, his hand trembling as he traced the strange sigils carved into the wall.

"No. No. No. This cannot be right," the old man muttered.

Hughe grabbed his arm and spun him around. "Where are they?"

Tears welled in the old man's eyes. "Beyond," he whispered. "Somewhere we cannot follow."

CHAPTER TEN

Everything was black. Then Dara and Avetta stood in a massive graveyard that stretched as far as they could see in every direction. A low mist clung to the ground, broken only by the endless crumbling headstones jutting like reefs from a leprous sea. It was eerily silent, the only sounds their own rapid breathing. The air was thick with a sulfurous, bog-like stench.

A dim, diffused light came from the sky, a sort of green twilight with no sun or moon visible.

"Where are we?" Avetta cried. "How did we get here?"

"I don't know," Dara answered grimly, her eyes searching the horizon. She slowly turned in a circle, looking for any sign of the cavern or tunnel they had left behind, but there was nothing except the endless necropolis.

A few feet away, the mist began to swirl and eddy as if something below were disturbing it.

"What is that?" Avetta's voice trembled.

They did not have to wait long for an answer. The mist thinned as something clawed its way out of the ground. Its head was covered in dirt, but Dara could clearly make out the same red blemish she had seen earlier.

Her sword was gone. Dara cursed and picked up a chunk of headstone. Before the ghoul could free itself from the earth, she bashed it in the head. Once, twice, three times—until it went still. She tossed the stone away. "Stay dead this time, damn you!" she snapped.

She turned to Avetta, taking her by the arm. "We need to get out of here."

***

They ran. How long, Dara couldn't tell, but her lungs ached.

"I can't," Avetta gasped hoarsely.

Dara stopped. "Catch your breath a moment, but then we keep going." She noticed something at the edge of the horizon—a lone black tower, needle-thin in the distance. She pointed toward it. "Just a little farther. We may be able to find help there, or at least a place to hide."

The pale-haired girl nodded, and they ran again for a time.

Dara sensed a change in the air. Glancing behind them, she saw a massive, indistinct dark shape rising into the sky.

They kept running, but Dara stole another glance backward. The silhouette was more void than shadow, but it moved, if only just. Unfathomably large, its outline was lost in the sheer madness of its scale, and it seemed to be advancing toward them.

Avetta dropped to the misty ground. "What do you keep looking at?" she asked between gasping breaths. "Whatever it is... I can't run anymore."

Dara grabbed her up by the arm and shook her. "We cannot stay here, and I cannot carry you. Please. We must reach that tower."

The girl nodded and began to lope along beside her.

Dara had the distinct feeling they were being watched from above by something other than the leviathan that was stalking them. She couldn't see it—but it was there.

"Faster!" she urged Avetta.

CHAPTER ELEVEN

"How is this going to help us find them?" Hughe asked, his frustration clearly mounting.

Tamir finished pouring a ring of salt large enough for him to sit inside.

"We cannot reach them in these bodies," the old man said, "but I may be able to find them another way." He seated himself within the circle, tucking his legs beneath him, hands resting lightly upon his chest.

Hughe looked doubtful. "Another spell to point us in the right direction?"

"This is a different sort of magic." Tamir inhaled slowly. "I have only attempted this twice in my life, and I have never completely left my body."

"What the devil does that mean?"

"Listen now!" the old man scolded. "The circle will keep spiritual forces away from my body, but I will need you to watch over it. Do not wake me, and do not let anything disturb me. I am going to try to send my spirit after them."

Tamir closed his eyes and began to chant in the old tongue, a singsong lilt lifting each verse. He bent his entire will toward expelling his spirit from his body.

After several moments, Tamir cursed in exasperation. "It is not working."

He opened his eyes and found his position in the room had shifted. He was looking at Hughe, Peter—and at himself.

The knight and the boy stared at his other self, who still sat within the circle.

A ghostly silver cord stretched between the center of his two selves.

"Do not let anything touch me," he said, but neither Hughe nor the boy gave any indication they had heard him.

Tamir turned toward the dead end with the strange sigils carved upon it. As he made to step forward, his legs moved, but his feet glided over the ground. He drifted swiftly toward the wall, instinctively putting out his hands to cushion the impact.

There was none, however. Instead, everything went black, and he felt as if he were being spun around and flipped upside down.

When he could see again, he stood in a misty graveyard that extended to infinity.

Movement in the distance caught his attention—two figures traveling in the opposite direction. On the horizon, beyond them, loomed a lone tower.

Tamir's ethereal heart leaped in his chest. *Could that be Dara and her companion?*

The old man took a step toward them, but the motion plucked him from the ground. When he tried to place his foot again, he only drifted higher. Each attempt lifted him farther and quickened his pace until he found himself gliding upward and forward, without any effort or control.

Tamir willed himself downward, but it did nothing to change his course. He could see now that it was indeed Dara and her companion, but at his current trajectory, he was going to completely overshoot them.

He cried out to Dara, "It is me! It is Tamir! Look up!"

Dara did look up then as he sailed over her head, but she did not answer and there was no sign of recognition in her expression.

"No!" Tamir cried, turning around in the air. He was still drifting away from the girls, heading in the same direction they were, toward the tower, but he would reach it well ahead of them. As he looked back, he saw the silver cord trailing endlessly behind him and vanishing into the mist.

Then he saw it. A thing that was and was not there, rising from the dreamlike landscape behind the girls. It moved like a vision half-formed—towering, bipedal, with too many arms, its body too vast to reconcile. It didn't walk so much as loom, its progress inexorable... as if the nightmarish realm had become self-aware.

Tamir cried out a warning to Dara that went unheard.

He was still being drawn away from them, but as he turned to glance at the approaching tower, he saw that it was more like an obelisk.

He began to panic. It looked as if Dara and her companion were making their way toward the same structure, but he was in danger of flying right over the top of it. The dark shape would overtake them any moment now.

Tamir closed his eyes and used all his will to force himself downward. *Down. Down. Down.* When he opened them again, he was suspended, motionless, about a foot above the top of the obelisk.

He struggled to change position until he was upside down. Reaching out, he tried to grasp the slender tip of the obelisk, hoping to use it to work his way down to the base.

But the stone passed right through his hands—and instead, he snagged the silver cord trailing from his middle. He released it, and it rebounded like a bowstring.

Tamir looked down. The girls had reached the base. They were desperately looking for a way inside. The dark shape loomed close behind them, swallowing the horizon.

His eyes raked over the structure, searching for an opening. He focused on the wall before the girls and, without knowing why, willed it to open.

To his amazement, it did.

The girls examined the opening for a moment, seemingly stunned. Then they stepped through and disappeared.

Encouraged, Tamir focused his will again, pouring everything into the desire to descend.

A strange sensation followed, as if he were falling headfirst. He opened his eyes and saw nothing—only blackness, rushing up to meet him as he fell.

CHAPTER TWELVE

The dark shape was close enough now to blot out the entire sky and the green twilight of the surrounding plane.

The heavy atmosphere practically hummed with silence, broken only by their own panting breaths. Dara and Avetta reached the base of the obelisk. It was much narrower than it had appeared at a distance. But if they could just get inside, it might at least offer some protection. There was no door, however, only a rectangular outline with no handles or locks.

"We need to get inside," Dara said.

"But how? There's no way in!"

"I don't know. Just try something." Dara blinked and the outline was gone, replaced by a yawning rectangle of inky darkness.

Avetta shook her head, her posture stiffening. "This isn't right."

"We don't have a choice." Dara seized her by the arm, yanking her forward. They plunged into the void and found themselves in a wide corridor that stretched into the distance. It was lined with peaked archways and lit torches, each flame steady and untouched by any draft.

Avetta's mouth gaped. "How?"

"It doesn't matter. We have to move."

CHAPTER THIRTEEN

Tamir could see again. A sickly ocher light oozed from a brazier in the center of a vast cavern. The walls and much of the floor were honeycombed with holes, just big enough for a man to crawl into... or out of.

Lone ghouls and small packs of the creatures loped around the cavern between piles of bones, their strange yipping sounds echoing overhead. None of them paid him any attention.

The scribe floated toward the far wall, his feet inches above the ground. He flinched as two ghouls passed through him, but he felt nothing. They continued, unaware of his presence, and climbed into one of the lightless holes.

There was a carving in the wall above the cavity, and he drifted closer to inspect it. It was an unfamiliar sigil, not in any script, magical or otherwise, that he recognized.

Tamir looked to the dark opening beside it and found that it too bore a sigil, different to the first. With a slight tilt of his head, he assumed a kneeling position while still hovering and scrutinized a small mound of red sand beneath the hole.

He studied the next nearest hollow and saw yet a third, distinct sigil carved above it. A faint whistling rose from within, and a sudden gust of wind blew dead leaves out of the shaft.

"They mark the various realms," said a voice from behind, startling him.

He turned and saw a man of perhaps thirty years, dressed in robes. Esoteric tattoos covered his hands, but though he looked more solid than the scribe's own limbs, he did not appear completely corporeal either. And unlike Tamir, the stranger's feet seemed to touch the ground.

"Who are you?" Tamir asked, studying the stranger intently.

"A traveler who came here long ago." He pointed to the silver cord now trailing from Tamir's back. "My anchor was severed, and I could not return to the waking world. I have been here ever since."

"Can you help me? There is a young woman who has come to be here in her physical body, along with another. I saw them enter this structure, but I lost them."

Silent, the man seemed to weigh the question.

"I need to find them and find a way back," Tamir pleaded. "We entered this place through a sort of eldritch gate, but I have not seen it here, on this side."

"Your anchor will guide you back to your body, but as for your friends... some gates into this realm only exist in the waking worlds."

Tamir's heart sank. "Then how can I take them home?"

The man gestured toward the holes. "These tunnels lead to the various material worlds."

"How will I know which is the right one? Can you read these sigils?"

"Not precisely, but I've been here a long time. Long enough to understand much of the ghouls' speech. With little else to do, I listen to them share tales of the realms they journey to. I've come to associate certain sigils with their destinations."

Tamir felt a sharp pain in his abdomen, but he ignored it. "Why haven't you found the portal that will take you home?"

The stranger sighed. "I have. But when my anchor was severed, my body perished. I have no physical form to return to. At least here, I remain myself." He glanced aside. "Where do you and your friends need to go?"

"A city called Thiardun. Do you know it?"

A distant look crossed the man's face. "I do."

"Show me, please, and I will go to them."

The stranger held up a hand. "I am afraid you would find they can neither hear nor see you. It took me a long time to master my spirit self."

Tamir uttered a silent curse, knowing the stranger was right. He raised his hand to his brow, despite himself, but his fingers met no resistance, as if he were smoke. “I tried to shout to her earlier, but she could not hear me. Then two ghouls passed through me as if I weren’t there. I cannot even move properly in the direction I wish to go. What can I do? She is like a daugh—” He cried out abruptly, a searing pain spreading through his center.

“What is wrong?” the man asked.

“It feels like something is gnawing on my insides.”

“You must return to your body quickly,” the man urged. “There are others who have been trapped here much longer than I, and it has driven them mad. They wish to sever your anchor so that you meet the same fate.”

“But I must find Dara!” Tamir grimaced and doubled over.

“I will find Dara and show her the way out. Now you must go before it is too late.”

“Tell her my name—” Tamir began, but the stranger reached out without warning and touched his forehead. The scribe felt as if he were filled with lightning. He was drawn backward as if by a strip of sinew stretched to its breaking point and then released, flying through the walls of the obelisk in an instant and over the misty landscape.

Glancing down, he saw a cluster of shadowy forms hunkered together in a single spot, growling and chittering as they vied for something between them. Looking closer, he saw it was his anchor they had pinned to the ground, the silvery cord now grimy and torn as they clawed and chewed it. And though it was some distance from him, he could feel every savage bite and ragged tear as if fangs and claws were sinking into his own belly.

As he flew past them, the cord grew taut again, and he began to decelerate. He turned to face the direction he was traveling and there hung a shimmering outline, like a portal. Knowing it must be the doorway back to the caverns beneath Thiardun, Tamir stretched his hands out toward it, willing himself forward, but he continued to slow. He was only a few feet away when he came to a complete halt.

He looked desperately toward the forms attacking his anchor, fearing they would sever it, leaving him stranded, never knowing if Dara truly made it home.

He grabbed hold of the cord with both hands and tried to tug it out of the shadow figures' grasp. It stretched, but they would not let go.

Tamir cried out in rage, and a blue light pulsed from his hands into the cord, racing down its length like a wave until it reached the figures. It pulsed again among them, and the shadows shrieked, turning the anchor loose as if they had been gripping hot pokers.

As soon as the shadows let go, the cord snapped taut once more and yanked Tamir toward the portal. He closed his eyes as he felt the familiar sensation of being spun through space and flipped end over end.

Then everything felt still, and he opened his eyes to find Hughe and Peter looking at him, faces etched with concern.

Tamir bowed his head and covered himself with his hands. "I had to leave them," he said mournfully.

CHAPTER FOURTEEN

"Hells!" Dara cursed, ripping a torch from its sconce and flinging it to the floor. She glanced around, scowling. "If I didn't know better, I'd swear we've already walked this same corridor—more than once." Then, catching the disheartened look on her companion's face, she softened. "Come on."

They made a right at the next intersection, and their mouths opened in surprise. At the far end of the new corridor, a guttering torch lay upon the ground.

"That's not possible." Avetta dug her nails into her arms, as if trying to wake herself.

"Come on!" Equally disturbed, Dara gestured for the girl to follow her back the way they had come.

They quickly retraced their steps and sharply turned the corner. There, a few feet away, lay a burning torch.

Avetta sank to the floor with her back to the wall of the corridor. "This is hopeless. We'll never find our way out of here." She covered her face with her hands and quietly wept.

Dara didn't have the strength to reproach the girl. There was no telling how long they'd wandered this endless place, where every turn brought them back to the same passage.

She squatted next to Avetta. Putting an arm around the girl's shoulders, she stroked her hair. "We'll find a way out."

Dara got the strong feeling they were being watched again. She raised her eyes slowly, trying not to alarm Avetta.

A few feet away, a man in robes stood, staring in their direction. His presence hadn't been announced by footsteps or any other sound. He was simply there.

"Avetta," she whispered, untangling herself from the embrace and rising warily to her feet.

"Don't be alarmed," the man said. He showed her his empty hands.

Dara's eyes narrowed. The outline of his robes was visible through his hands, and beyond them, the corridor, as if he were no more substantial than a thin veil of smoke.

"Hells," Dara exhaled warily. "Are you some kind of ghost?"

"In a manner of speaking, I suppose I am." His tone was calm and reassuring, but Dara pulled Avetta to her feet and ushered her behind herself as she took a step backward.

He took a step toward them. "Is one of you named Dara?"

Dara halted abruptly. "How do you know my name?"

"An old man asked me to find you."

Taking another step backward, Dara asked, "Did this old man have a name?"

"I did not have a chance to ask it. He was here in spirit only, and I had to send him back to his body before he became trapped here forever."

Her brow arched. "Why did this old man want you to find me?"

"To show you the way home," he said with quiet reassurance.

Could it really be...? Dara caught her lower lip between her teeth and weighed their options.

They could take a chance on this mysterious spirit who claimed to want to help them, his true motivations known only to himself—or they could keep wandering until they stumbled into something worse.

She scoffed. The gods were a lie, but hungry corpses and whispering shades were real enough. And if those were real, perhaps a benevolent spirit guide could be too.

Dara turned to Avetta and gave the girl what she hoped was a reassuring smile, then nodded once. The girl returned the gesture, uncertainty clouding her face.

Dara gave the spirit a sideways glance. "All right. Show us the way home."

Their ghostly guide beckoned, and they followed him down a corridor that branched into a shorter passage. The end of this passage opened into a vast cavern beyond.

"How?" Dara demanded. "We've been wandering for hours, and every turn just brought us back to the same passage."

"Things are different in the Idir." He halted and favored her with a sad smile. "In this place, the path is inconsequential if you do not know the destination."

They stood at the threshold of the cavern. It reminded Dara of a representation of hell she had once seen in the stained glass of a temple. Ironic, since she'd been there to rob it. There were bones in the cavern—and countless ghouls.

"I'm not going in there," Avetta blurted out, wide-eyed.

"What trick is this?!" Dara snarled.

"Keep quiet," he warned. "There is no trick. Those holes are tunnels. Gateways the ghouls use to pass between this place and the material worlds. Their exits lie in neglected burial grounds, forgotten battlefields, and other forsaken places. The old man said you came from Thiardun, and I know of a tunnel that leads there. Though in truth, I cannot say exactly where in Thiardun it will take you."

"This is madness," Avetta challenged. "Why should we trust him?"

Dara turned to the spirit. "Why *are* you helping us?"

The spirit grew melancholy. "I came here long ago, much like the old man, looking for those I cared about who had been lost to this place. In the end, I was too late to help them, but perhaps what befell me doesn't have to be for naught."

Dara turned toward the younger woman and met her gaze. "Come Avetta. I believe he is telling the truth."

Avetta hesitated, studying Dara. "I'll follow you," she said finally.

The spirit looked at each of them for a moment. "Once we enter the cavern, you must move as swiftly as you can. You cannot let them catch you. I will show you the tunnel you must take." He turned to enter the cavern.

"What is your name?" Dara asked gently.

The spirit turned back and sighed. "It *was* Branoc."

Dara gave him a soft smile. "Thank you, Branoc."

She swallowed and grasped Avetta's hand, her gaze flicking to the cavern beyond. They followed him inside with hurried steps. His footfalls were silent, but theirs echoed loudly.

All around the cavern, ghouls were turning to stare at them as they ran. Then, as one, the lot of them began to lope toward them.

"Hurry!" Branoc urged. "The tunnel you seek is right there," He pointed. "Do not hesitate!"

Sprinting toward the unnatural network of hollows, the mass of grave spawn bounding after them closed the distance.

They reached the hole their guide indicated just ahead of their pursuers. Dara shoved Avetta inside before following directly behind.

"Turn back, foul things," they heard Branoc shout, his voice ringing out loud and defiant. He hurled a rebuke in an unknown tongue: "*Trawch Amath, Guthraelydd Ffaeth. Genwch Unrhiw Erbidd.*" Then his speech shifted into something that sounded even older: "*Darak Zulmu, Gidin Eshgal Zu* Millenoth!"

"Don't stop!" Dara shouted. The tunnel was barely wide enough for them to scramble on all fours, and they clawed through the pitch dark as fast as they could, damp earth pressing into their noses and mouths. Though Branoc had bought them a moment, she could still hear the creatures clawing closer. She imagined hot breath on her ankles.

Dara was brought to a sudden halt by Avetta's feet blocking her way.

"What are you doing?!" Dara shouted, panic in her voice.

As the echoes of her words faded, she heard the cacophony behind her growing louder—the frantic scrabbling of clawed hands and feet almost upon them.

Avetta gasped raggedly up ahead.

"There is a second tunnel opening! I don't know which one!"

There was no time to ponder the choice. Dara shoved Avetta's foot hard.

"It doesn't matter! Pick one or we die!"

The girl began to move again, and Dara pushed her onward as she hurried behind.

Then a sudden change in pressure filled the tunnel, and Dara had to resist the urge to cover her ears.

Avetta shrieked.

Dara reached out, but she could no longer feel the girl's feet. Instead, she felt the edges of another hole ahead of her. It was tight and she had to squeeze herself through. When she did, she felt the brittle bones of a skeleton beneath her. She was no longer within the confines of the narrow tunnel, and she found that she was able to rise to a crouch.

The sound of something slobbering and grunting in the tunnel they had just quit reached Dara's ears. She snatched up one of the bones she had just crawled over and drove it into the face of the first ghoul trying to claw its way in.

"I think I found some kind of door!" Avetta shouted. "It's too heavy. I need your help to open it!"

Dara shoved against the dead ghoul in the tunnel exit, using it to hold back the snarling fiends behind it. In the oppressive blackness, she couldn't see the door Avetta was trying to open. If she let go to join the girl, the ghouls would pour through. But if she didn't, it was only a matter of moments before they were torn to shreds anyway.

With a guttural curse, she lunged toward the girl's voice and threw her weight against the unseen door.

CHAPTER FIFTEEN

Hughe followed Tamir up the stairs to the loft above his shop. He moved to take a seat in the chair next to the railing, but the older man stopped him, placing a firm but gentle hand on the knight's arm.

"Not there," Tamir said. His tone was somber, his red eyes shadowed within dark, sunken flesh. "That is hers."

Hughe nodded. "Forgive me."

"Not at all. Take mine," Tamir said, gesturing toward the overstuffed chair opposite Dara's seat.

Tamir dragged a wooden stool from behind his worktable and sat across from the knight. A long moment of silence passed as Hughe struggled to find the right place to begin.

Finally, he said, "They have filled the tunnel where she disappeared with stones and walled off the entrance."

"Damn them!" Tamir slammed his fist against his leg and rose, ready to storm down the stairs.

"Wait," Hughe said earnestly. "We stayed there for two nights ourselves with no sign of her, and it has been another three since the city watch took over. If she were coming back..." He hesitated. "At least if she were coming back there, she would have already done so."

The knight stood and placed a hand on Tamir's shoulder. "Please sit."

An inner struggle waged war behind the old man's eyes for a moment before he sank back onto the stool with hunched shoulders and a downcast face.

Hughe continued. "The seneschal, Corgrith, and the others' bodies still haven't been found. Thank Millenoth we took that poor girl's body with us when we left. Otherwise, she would never have a proper burial."

Tamir looked up. "And what have the *authorities* surmised about the coin-master's involvement?"

Hughe exhaled slowly. "The secret chambers below his estate told enough of a tale that they couldn't dispute everything we recounted to them. However, I've been forbidden from ever speaking of it again. I was told in no uncertain terms that if I were to violate this order, I would not only be publicly discredited, but the verdict on my involvement in the fight in the alley last week would swiftly change from self-defense to murder."

"Bastards! Well, they will not stop me from spreading the truth from one end of this damned city to the other!"

The knight glanced away before meeting Tamir's furious stare. "I'm to give you a message that if you speak of what happened to anyone, you will be charged with sedition."

"Let them hang me for all that I care!" The old man's eyes burned.

Hughe studied the scribe. He understood his pain and anger. How could he convince him not to throw his life away pointlessly?

The sound of the front door slamming shut broke the silence, startling them. "You left the door unlocked again, old man," called a familiar female voice from below.

Both men sprang to their feet and peered over the railing with shocked expressions on their faces.

There stood Dara and the pale-haired girl they had last seen her with. Both were filthy, their torn clothing caked with dried mud. Dara's smile belied the tears in her eyes.

Tamir rushed down the stairs with Hughe right behind. The old man embraced her so aggressively that he nearly knocked her from her feet.

Hughe gave a nod to the girl beside her. She looked exhausted but unharmed.

Through her tears, Dara scolded both men, "How did you get back here and get cleaned up so fast? Shouldn't you be out looking for us?"

"Dara," Hughe responded in an uncertain tone, "you've been missing for five days."

Her companion shook her head slowly. "But that's impossible."

Dara frowned, pulling free from Tamir. "What do you mean? We broke out of a crypt at dawn—this morning."

The knight's eyes narrowed. "That may be, but days have passed since we last saw you. Much has happened since then."

Tamir interjected. "It is true, child. Time must move differently in the other place. I was there so briefly that we did not notice it."

"So, it *was* you Branoc was talking about." She hugged the old man again.

"Branoc?" Hughe asked.

Tamir answered, "He must have been the trapped soul I told you about. He kept his word, after all." His gaze lingered on Dara, a mix of wonder and disbelief flooding his face as tears began to brim in his eyes.

As if she wanted to spare him any embarrassment over the display of emotion, Dara nodded. "Enough talk for now. One day or five, we need something to drink and some food. And I'm sure Avetta would appreciate a proper bath before she sees her family."

"Of course," Tamir agreed. He turned and forced a cough into his sleeve while using it to dab inconspicuously at his face.

Hughe swallowed the lump forming in his own throat. "I have to report for duty," he said with reluctance. "Please don't relate the truth of what happened to anyone."

Tamir turned back and started to protest.

"For all our sakes," Hughe warned.

The old man looked at Dara, his expression softening. "Agreed."

Hughe headed for the door, but Dara tugged at his tunic. He turned to find her looking at him intently. No amount of dirt could diminish her charm.

"Thank you." Her green eyes pierced him.

"You're welcome," he said, clearing his throat as the words settled heavier than he expected.

He glanced aside, then added with a crooked smile, "After all... I couldn't very well walk around in your debt, could I?"

He hesitated, then reached out and tucked a stray lock of her hair behind her ear.

Dara tilted her head slightly, a faint smirk on her lips. "No. That would be... terribly inconvenient."

BENEATH THE BLACK KEEP

CHAPTER ONE

The grizzled Yidwyr and his charge sat opposite each other at an unfinished pine table, near the center of the small, country tavern. Both wore leather tunics, their boots caked with dirt and their tattered cloaks draped over their packs on the benches next to them.

Late afternoon sunlight streamed through the open shutters, filling the room. It smelled like a dozen other taverns they'd stopped in during their travels—smoke, damp wool, and the sharp tang of men who worked the fields.

The other patrons, mostly farmers, had thus far refrained from approaching them, but the pair had heard the familiar moniker, Silvermen, several times already amid the whispers and muted gossip surrounding them.

Their journey had begun at Caer Argyn, the coastal fortress of the Galani Yidwyr, where Owyn's training had also commenced, and then carried them eastward across the breadth of Gauldün. This evening, they found themselves in a frontier village less than a couple of days' ride from the untamed lands of Besh.

The thought of those ancient forests and wild, barbarian tribes stirred Owyn's sense of adventure.

Owyn had close-cropped sandy hair and eyes too soft for a boy in training to face the dead. He was fifteen, average in height, with the lean, wiry frame of an active youth. Tearing a chunk of bread from the loaf set between them, he looked up to find his master watching him with a critical expression.

Bledig was in his sixties, with a hoary mane of hair and a stubbly beard. The backs of his hands were covered in tattoos, a fusion of runes and esoteric religious symbols.

The boy dunked his bread into his soup with exaggerated care, feigning concentration and trying to appear deep in thought. At times like this, when his master wore a stern countenance, something which occurred far too often for Owyn's liking, the last thing he wanted to do was invite conversation. That would only lead to a test and, inevitably, to disappointment.

Nearly a year under Bledig's charge, and each daybreak brought fresh certainty: His master would send him back to the nuns who'd raised him. That would be more than he could bear. Besides the shame of failure, he was simply too old for the nuns to know what to do with him anymore.

He scoffed to himself. He did every chore Bledig gave him without complaint and spent hours at sword drills, but nothing ever elicited a word of praise from his master. Instead, the old Silverman hammered him constantly with questions about symbols, mystic rituals, the properties of various herbs, and on and on.

"Wyrmwort?" Bledig asked without warning, cutting through the tavern's low hum.

Owyn chewed slowly to buy time. There were so many damned herbs. He answered tentatively, "Brew a pinch in your tea... it bolsters courage."

He looked for a flicker of approval. Bledig gave none, but he didn't correct him either. Owyn's shoulders relaxed.

"Aylruna?" the old man prompted.

Owyn replied more confidently, "Useful for luring grave spawn into traps. 'Draws 'em like flies to honey.'" He grinned, pleased with himself that he'd recalled his master's exact words.

But Bledig was already reaching into his pack. Two pouches appeared. Correct answers, as always, only brought harder questions.

Bledig upended the pouches and spilled two small piles onto the table. One pile had purplish stems, and leaves that were green on top, with fine white hairs lining the undersides. The other, yellow stems and tiny red leaves.

Owyn stared at them and bit his lip.

The Silverman's eyes narrowed. "If you must think about it, it's too late. The dead won't wait for you to consult the grimoire."

He tried to home in on the scent of either herb, to separate it from the other odors in the crowded tavern. He thought he caught a bitter, almost sage-like aroma from the red leaves. Hesitantly, Owyn pointed to the purple-stemmed pile first. "Aylruna." He then pointed at the other. "Wyrmwort."

Bledig shook his head.

Owyn slumped, watching as the herbs were swept back into their pouches.

When Bledig spoke again, there was a softer edge to his voice, but the words still stung. "You're too old to go back to the nuns, but still young enough to find something else. A proper trade. A forge. You're a strong-enough lad. I know a blacksmith who'd treat you well."

Owyn stared past him, unseeing. He imagined a life at the forge. Sweat, heat, and repetition. Day after day. The thought crushed something in him.

He blinked. Three local lads stood near the kitchen, glaring at him. He saw the tallest of the three cast a glance toward the bar and followed his gaze to where a fair-haired serving girl loaded mugs onto a tray. To Owyn's surprise, she was looking right at him.

She smiled.

He returned a bewildered smile of his own before remembering the hostile expressions on the faces of the others. When he glanced back their way, he could tell the exchange with the girl was not lost on them. They scowled.

Bledig, oblivious to the exchange, continued, "You've never faced the dead, boy. That's why I've brought you here, so far from Caer Argyn. To give you a taste of the fear without putting you in real danger."

This last statement brought Owyn's attention back to the conversation at hand. "Give me a taste of *what*?"

"There is a deserted keep a few leagues to the east. In the catacombs beneath it, imprisoned for more than a century, lies a thing of pure evil." Bledig paused and watched the boy's face carefully.

Gooseflesh rose on Owyn's arms. He leaned forward and asked in an earnest tone, "If it is already imprisoned, why go there?"

Bledig's expression softened. "So you can feel it. Its presence. We'll stay above ground, but you'll know it's there. If afterward, you decide this is not your calling, there is no shame in that."

Owyn sat back and folded his arms. "I'm not afraid."

Bledig gave an impatient wave of his hand. "It is wise to fear such things." He rose from the table. "I need to use the privy. Finish your supper before I get back." Having said that, he made his way to the door.

Owyn stared at the table.

"Hello," said a pleasant voice.

He looked up. The girl was there, smiling at him. Close up, he could see her eyes were the color of honey, and her cheeks were lightly dusted with freckles. She was a year, maybe two, older than he was.

He felt the blush rise in his cheeks as he smiled back. Outside of the nuns, he hadn't had many opportunities to talk to the fairer sex.

"I'm Briann," she said.

"My name is Owyn," he replied, his voice cracking as he spoke. He felt his face grow hotter.

She giggled. "Are you really Silvermen?" she asked with a mischievous gleam in her eyes.

"Yes... we ah... well, my master is. I'm not quite yet," Owyn stammered.

She appeared both surprised and impressed by this. "Oh. I was only teasing, but you really are, aren't you? Is it true that you live in a silver keep?"

"Caer Argyn? No, not really. It's just gray stone."

"Oh." Her expression dimmed. "Are your swords silver, then?"

"No." He laughed. "A silver sword would be ruined pretty quickly in a fight."

She looked mildly disappointed.

He was about to explain how the Galani Yidwyr of old had carried silver chains with them to bind ghouls, but he could see her attention drifting back toward the bar, and he stopped himself.

"Bledig does have a silver dagger," he offered quickly.

Her eyebrows lifted. "Indeed?"

"Silver's a scourge to most grave spawn," he said, trying not to sound too eager.

She smiled again. Encouraged, he pointed subtly at the tall boy still glaring at him. "Is that your betrothed?"

Briann looked confused. "Betrothed?" She turned to see who Owyn was referring to and laughed. "No. Martin is a friend." Her face turned somber. "There were two men here last night, strangers, asking rude questions. I told Martin about them, and I think he thinks he is looking after me."

"I'm glad to hear it," Owyn responded. "Not that someone was rude to you, of course," he said awkwardly. "I mean that Martin is your friend." He blinked. "I mean that he is looking after you."

Briann laughed, eyes bright with mischief again. "I know what you meant."

It made him happy to hear her laugh, even if it was at his expense.

Bledig reappeared and sat down, his presence instantly severing Owyn's fleeting connection with Briann.

"Well," she said, and curtsied to Bledig. "I must get back to work now." She turned and hurried back to the bar.

Owyn sighed and rested his chin on his fist.

Bledig frowned at him. "I'm going to tarry a bit longer. You go and check on the horses. I'll meet you at the inn."

Owyn shook his head as he gathered up his things, replaying his brief conversation with Briann as he left the tavern.

CHAPTER TWO

The moon was up when Owyn emerged from the stable. He started down the curved dirt path, screened on both sides by beech trees. Though he was headed for the inn, what he really wanted was to go back to the tavern.

He'd taken only a few paces down the dirt path when he heard booted feet rushing up close behind him. He turned to look—but too late. A foot hooked his leg, and he was shoved hard to the ground. His head hit when he landed.

Flat on his back, he pushed up on his elbows to see figures standing over him: the three youths from the tavern.

"You've overstayed your welcome in Dunbrook," the tall one, *Martin*, said, his lips curled back from clenched teeth.

Owyn got unsteadily to his feet. The ground seemed to tilt around him for a moment, but he rose to his full height and the world finally righted itself.

Martin and the boy on his left were empty-handed, but the one on his right brandished a wooden cudgel.

"You attacked me from behind," Owyn said, full of indignation. "What kind of coward does that?"

"Did you hear what I said? Leave!" Martin's face reddened.

The young Silverman slapped dust from his tunic. "I don't think I will, just yet, but I'm curious—how is that your business?"

Owyn didn't wait for an answer. He lunged forward and caught Martin by surprise, cracking him in the nose with a sharp jab.

***

Dust flew. Fists landed with dull thuds. Boots scraped and slid across the path. For a moment, none of the gathering onlookers could say who was winning.

When the dust began to settle, it revealed two of the youths restraining Owyn by his arms as Martin loomed in front of him. The taller boy balled his fist and cocked it back, aimed at Owyn's face.

***

Bledig grumbled to himself as he watched the stampede of locals rush from the tavern. He sighed and followed, muttering under his breath. Maybe it would have been wiser to make camp under the stars.

Outside, a male voice bellowed in pain. He hurried toward the commotion and pushed his way through the onlookers to see three bloodied youths sprawled on their backs. Owyn stood over them, blood on his own face and a cudgel in his hand. One boy writhed in the dirt, moaning in agony and clutching a broken wrist against his chest.

Bledig's brow arched with fleeting surprise at the boy's fire. Still, this would not sit well with the locals. His eyes narrowed and he frowned at Owyn.

***

With the tavern suddenly emptied, Briann was alone. Shaking her head, she spotted an overturned mug near the edge of a table. She picked it up and began wiping up the spilled wine when a creak came from behind the bar.

She walked toward the bar, set the mug down, and looked toward the kitchen. The door to the kitchen was propped open, as usual. Through it, she could see the back door. It was closed.

Briann shrugged and headed back between the tables to right a chair that had also been knocked over when the patron occupying it had made his hasty exit from the tavern. As she bent to straighten the chair, something rasped softly behind the bar, like leather dragged across wood.

She moved quickly. If a rat had gotten in somehow, she wanted to be rid of it before the patrons returned.

Rounding the bar, she was startled to find a man crouched there. He smiled as he stood, and she recognized him as one of the rude strangers from the night before.

Briann grabbed the mug from the bar top, ready to pitch it at his head, but before she could, someone grabbed her from behind.

A hand clamped over her mouth, forcing a damp cloth to her face. Her eyes went wide, but her scream was smothered. A strong arm circled her waist and held her fast. She was still conscious but unable to resist as she was dragged backward toward the kitchen—and the back door.

CHAPTER THREE

Owyn and Bledig walked their horses across the moonlit heath, their breath visible in the chill air.

"We could be asleep in warm beds back at the inn instead of trudging through the moors in the dark," Owyn protested under his breath.

"The middle of the night isn't how I would have preferred to enter the keep either," Bledig said. "But we couldn't very well spend the night in the village after you broke the arm of the elder's boy. Not if we don't want our throats cut in our sleep."

Owyn's brow furrowed. "I didn't start it. They attacked me."

"So you've said."

They reached the top of a small rise and looked down into a shallow basin. Shadowed husks of what was once a village were splayed out across the bottom. Just beyond the far edge of the ruins, a lone hill rose above the surrounding terrain.

Atop the hill sat a black fortress. Framed against the night sky in the moonlight, the battlements resembled exposed vertebrae. Imposingly high walls enclosed the towers and central keep. The whole structure gave the impression of an ancient gargoyle come to life, waiting to pounce.

After studying the fortress for a long moment, Owyn's gaze returned to the gloomy bones of the dead village, and he pulled his cloak tighter around his shoulders—because of the cold, he told himself.

They descended into the hollow. As they neared the ruins, stone foundations, and the remnants of charred wooden frames, preserved by the same fires that had gutted the structures, Owyn felt a deep melancholy begin to grip him.

"What happened here?" he asked somberly.

Bledig continued walking as he spoke. "More than a hundred years ago, when Gauldün was engaged in some of the fiercest fighting with the kingdom of Besh, one of King Eremon's most feared and brutal commanders was Odo the Black."

The pair began to weave their way in between the ruins as Bledig continued. "Odo and his retainers were so successful at conquering Beshan armies and holding territory won from them, that he was rewarded with the title of viscount and given the land we now walk upon."

Bledig glanced at Owyn as if to confirm the boy was listening. "During one of many temporary truces with Besh, this one lasting several years, a village developed here. But Odo was not content to sit in peace or fit to have stewardship over those who settled here. After a time, with no Beshan military blood to shed, his retainers began abducting villagers and taking them into the dungeons beneath the keep. Odo, it turned out, was a sadist and a torturer."

Owyn was so transfixed by Bledig's tale that he failed to avoid a large chunk of stone in his path. He stumbled, startling his horse, but managed to stay on his feet. Bledig paused and Owyn felt the color rise in his cheeks.

"Mind your steps," Bledig cautioned before continuing. "Some of the villagers eventually fled and brought word of their suffering to the High Priest of Millenoth, the Theomant. They claimed Odo had taken to worshipping a demon.

"The Theomant dispatched priests and a force of knights loyal to the church to investigate. When they arrived, the village was deserted. What they found beneath the keep was enough to condemn Odo and his retainers to death. The Theomant would have burned them at the stake and scattered their ashes. But because of his past victories against Besh, Odo still had the king's favor. The high priest was granted permission to execute Odo and his retainers, but he was forbidden to destroy their bodies or deny their wish for interment in the foul crypts beneath the keep."

Owyn's jaw went slack. "Surely he did not grant that wish."

Bledig nodded. "Gauldün has always honored the wishes of the dead and permitted the worship of other gods, even with the Church of Millenoth so prominent. Only after Odo did the laws change, banning hidden cults and secret rites."

"What did the Theomant do?" Owyn asked, enthralled by the lurid details of Bledig's tale.

"Despite Odo's many crimes and atrocities, the high priest complied with the king's edict. He didn't burn them at the stake, but he did command that their eyes be burned out with boiling oil before they were hanged. Their bodies were then entombed beneath the keep. As a precaution, he also instructed the priests and knights to build a wall over the entrance to the burial vault, and they covered it with holy wards to ensure Odo could never escape, should he rise from the dead. Then they burned the village to the ground."

They reached the bottom of the hill just as Bledig finished the tale. A narrow switchback path led up its face to a gatehouse. Bledig tethered their horses to a blackened, nearly horizontal beam which leaned against a wall of piled stones. They climbed the trail, boots crunching gravel with each step.

At the top of the path, a drawbridge spanned a dry, narrow gorge between them and the gatehouse. The night was eerily quiet; the only sounds that met their ears were those of their footsteps and the creaking planks of the drawbridge beneath them as they crossed it.

Owyn set an unlit lantern on the ground next to his pack and retrieved a pint of oil from it.

Bledig shook his head. "We'll want the corpse wax instead."

Owyn's eyes grew large at the implication, but he replaced the flask with a terracotta lamp and a glass jar. Removing the jar's lid, he grimaced as he scooped some of the waxy substance from within and dropped it into the lamp. He inserted a wick into the wax and set about lighting it with flint and steel. Soon, a soft yellow flame danced about the wick.

They resumed walking, and as they crossed the threshold of the gatehouse, entering the courtyard, Owyn's eyebrows rose. The lamp's flame burned blue.

"Does that mean…?"

"Aye. Spirits abound here," Bledig answered. "Many are the tormented souls of those tortured and murdered by Odo. But there are other, more sinister things here as well. As we walk the grounds and halls, you'll feel your hair stand on end and your guts shift. You may even see a spirit if one decides to manifest. But no harm will come to you; the real evil is beneath the keep, held at bay with runes and wards."

As Bledig finished speaking, a rumble resonated from within the northeastern tower at the other end of the courtyard, a sound like heavy stone grinding against stone. Owyn's face grew pale, even in the wan light from the blue lamp flame.

"Courage," Bledig chided. "Or will you let the echoes and phantom lights of this place destroy your resolve so soon?"

"I'm not afraid." Owyn's voice cracked. His mouth was dry, and his tongue stuck to the roof of his mouth.

Determined to prove he wasn't as frightened as he sounded, he began walking toward the tower and his master followed, letting the boy lead.

They passed the open portal of an outbuilding against the wall of the fortress and Owyn had the strong feeling that something was watching him from within the darkness of the structure. But he was determined not to lose face again in front of Bledig, and he kept it to himself.

About twenty paces from the tower's open entrance, a yellow light began to radiate from its floor, slowly rising into the air. Owyn glanced quickly at the lamp in his hand, but to his surprise the flame was no longer blue, just a mundane yellow.

Bledig grabbed him roughly by the shoulder. "That's no phantom," he said in a harsh whisper.

The sound of shod feet crunching gravel came from behind them then. Owyn turned to see two figures in dark, hooded robes approaching. Blades glinted from the wide sleeves of their robes.

Bledig drew his longsword from its scabbard with a menacing rasp of metal and turned to face the threat. Owyn looked back toward the tower and saw several other robed figures emerging. One carried a lantern. All wore strange, obsidian amulets around their necks.

"Cultists!" Bledig hissed. "Show them some steel, boy."

Owyn obliged and drew his sword. The pair stood back-to-back; Owyn facing the two who had emerged from the outbuilding and Bledig facing the four headed toward them from the tower.

Clinking chains and the grinding of rusted gears sounded from the gatehouse. The drawbridge began to rise, sealing them within the courtyard. Two more robed figures stepped out from the shadows of the darkened gatehouse.

The mysterious figures ran at them with blades bared.

Bledig just had enough time to whisper, "If you see an opening, run!" Then the fight was upon them. Their longswords clanged against sabers and daggers.

Owyn found himself separated from Bledig in the melee, barely holding off two attackers, retreating with every clash. Though he had spent much time practicing, this was his first real swordfight against someone trying to take his life.

Dancing backward and gaining some distance from his foes, he caught sight of Bledig just as the Silverman slashed open one man's guts. Another lay sprawled in the dust. Yet four more pressed against his guard. They lacked skill, but numbers gave them the advantage.

Owyn batted aside the dagger of an opponent, and his blade pierced the man's breast. The boy's eyes grew wide with the realization of what he had done. He'd romanticized killing an enemy hundreds of times while practicing, but now he was paralyzed by the shock of it, leaving himself vulnerable to the dagger of the other cultist facing him.

Owyn realized his peril too late, but before his attacker could strike, the tip of Bledig's sword burst from his chest. The old Silverman had seen what was about to happen and intervened.

It was Bledig who had left himself open now, however, and one of the robed figures quickly took advantage of it, sinking a dagger into his back.

"Bledig!" Without a thought, Owyn slashed Bledig's assailant through the throat, dropping him, gurgling, to the ground.

"Get the others!" one of the cultists shouted. Another responded by running back to the northeast tower.

The last two cautiously approached the boy where he knelt next to his master, searching underneath the Silverman's cloak until his fingers touched the smooth, walnut handle.

Owyn leveled the crossbow and fired. A cultist staggered two steps with a bolt lodged in his chest before his body hit the courtyard floor.

Bledig was unconscious. Owyn dropped the crossbow and pulled his master's arm around his neck. Placing his other arm underneath Bledig's, he lifted him to his feet.

Owyn managed to keep his sword pointed at the remaining cultist as he retreated toward the southeast tower, dragging Bledig along with him.

The cultist followed, warily keeping his distance from the boy's blade.

Owyn backed into the doorway, but his heels caught on the threshold. He fell hard, Bledig's weight driving the breath from his lungs.

Seeing the boy pinned, the cultist darted forward.

With a desperate heave, Owyn rolled Bledig aside, his boot catching the edge of the door. As the cultist lunged, he kicked it shut—right into the attacker's face.

Rising quickly, he groped around the doorframe in the dark. A muffled moan came from the other side.

"Over there!" someone shouted from the courtyard. The crunch of gravel followed as many booted feet swiftly approached.

Owyn found a wooden beam and fumbled it into the brackets. He hoped it would hold. He picked up his sword from the floor and held it indecisively for a few heartbeats before sheathing it.

The dark space stank of rotted sawdust and damp wood. A few slivers of moonlight slipped past the edges of the door. He looked around desperately, his eyes adjusting to the darkness just enough to make out the outline of the room.

Recognizing the silhouettes of a dozen or more bunkbeds, he realized he was in a small barracks. To his dismay, no other exits were visible.

"Let us in, boy! You've already caused enough trouble. You can die quick... or we can give you to *him*."

Owyn rushed toward the bunks. He knew it wouldn't take long for them to break through.

CHAPTER FOUR

Owyn's back and shoulders strained as he pushed against the bunk, forcing it across the stone floor with a loud scrape. He braced it against the door beside Bledig, who was slumped unconscious in a seated position against the wall. Finished with that task, he turned and rushed to the next nearest bunk. Though faint light filtered around the doorframe, enough to make out the rough shapes of the larger furniture, Owyn failed to see the small trunk in his path.

He crashed to the floor, his body slamming into the cold stone with a grunt. He managed to catch himself with his hands, but the impact jarred his wrists painfully. Groaning quietly, he pushed himself up, feeling the sting in his abraded palms.

Sharp whacks rang out against the door. Someone was attacking it with an axe. Owyn staggered to his feet, his breath quickening. He needed to find a spear or polearm—something longer than his sword. Something he could use to fight at a distance with, striking at them through the bunk frame. But he would need more light if he hoped to locate such a weapon without braining himself on the floor.

Owyn removed his pack and knelt. Rummaging around inside the pack in the near-dark, he felt the familiar shape of his tinderbox. The assault on the door echoed through the room as he fumbled the strike of flint against steel, his trembling hands failing on his first few attempts.

He stopped and drew in a long slow breath to steady himself. When he tried again, he struck true and the charcloth ignited, glowing faintly in the dimness.

He lit the candle stub from the tinderbox and raised it high, the weak flame casting shadows across the room. Owyn scanned the space, searching for the ideal weapon.

But something in the way the candle flame flickered caught his attention. Owyn studied it, confused, as the flame moved erratically, bending toward the wall behind him. He turned toward the wall and brought the candle closer. As he did so, the flame danced for a second before bending toward the wall once more.

Owyn examined the stones and mortar lines. Setting the candle down, he pushed against the wall. At first, nothing happened. Fresh sweat broke upon his brow. With a grinding sound, a square panel of stones swung inward, revealing an opening large enough for him to crawl into.

He lifted the candle again. He could see a tunnel, roughly three feet wide and four feet tall, finished in worked stone, extending far beyond his dim light.

A shower of splinters rained inward from the door as the axeblade bit through near the top. Owyn cast a desperate glance to where Bledig sat against the far wall. He knew there was no way he could drag his master across the room before the cultists forced their way in.

Sick in his stomach from his decision, Owyn crouched and waddled into the passage. He reached back and dragged his pack in after himself, managing to swing the false section of wall back into place just as the door on the other side of the room burst inward and several hands shoved the bunk bed aside.

CHAPTER FIVE

Owyn shuffled forward. The passage curved in a wide spiral that sloped downward. The descent was steep but not steep enough to put him in danger of losing his footing. His candle was burning low, and he knew it wouldn't last much longer. Soon he lost all perception of which direction north lay or even how far below the keep he might be.

The slope abruptly leveled off at a T-shaped junction. The height of the tunnel in the right-hand passage was enough that he could stand without crouching and so he chose to go in that direction.

The candle flame flickered weakly, desperately clinging to life before finally sputtering out, plunging Owyn into darkness.

Panic started to rise in his chest, but he remembered Bledig's training. Slowly drawing in and letting out several breaths, he felt reason return. He still had his tinderbox and two jars of lamp oil, but he had lost his lantern and the terracotta lamp.

Owyn reached out cautiously, afraid of what might be lurking in the black tunnel. The passage was narrow enough that his fingers could touch both the cold left and right walls at the same time. He took another slow deep breath, nodded to himself once, and began to move forward again.

After an indeterminable amount of time had passed, his right hand reached into a void. He carefully brought himself to the entrance of an intersecting passage and began to feel his way along in that direction. Owyn shivered; the tunnel was much cooler than the others.

This happened several more times, sometimes with the discovery of another right-hand passage and sometimes a left. He took the turns as he found them, hoping luck would lead him somewhere better.

More than once, he walked face first into a thick cobweb and swatted frantically, trying to drive off the hordes of imagined spiders.

A distant thundering reached his ears. He stopped and listened.

Echoing down the passage came the dull hammering of iron on stone—two or three strikes, then the crash of rubble. After a pause, it began again.

As he stood there listening, his eyes began to discern a rectangular entrance to a larger chamber, faintly limned with light, its source undeterminable.

Cautiously, Owyn crept forward. The pounding continued, each series of blows ending in a heavy crash of stone hitting the ground.

As he slunk deeper, his eyes adjusted to the gloom. The vault beyond the cramped passage was vast but lay in almost total blackness. Only the faint glow seeping around a pillar far ahead revealed anything at all.

The glow hinted at pillars to either side, the walls lost somewhere beyond, impossible to gauge. A broad colonnade seemed to divide the chamber ahead, and he followed this path toward the thudding hammers.

A feeling of being watched grew. He spun, searching desperately in the dark, but nothing moved.

He tilted his gaze upward, but the ceiling was smothered in darkness. He squinted, straining to make out any hidden detail. His breath caught. Sweat trickled down his spine. Something scuttled above. Something large. Owyn could only sense its bulk and motion as it traversed the ceiling, moving toward the other side of the vault in the same direction he was headed.

Owyn kept darting glances upward as he crept on. The glow from the obstructed source was much stronger now, and he could see an intersection where another colonnade of pillars crossed the vault, perpendicular to the one he was treading. He edged closer to the light.

"This ought to be enough," said a deep voice.

The man who answered sounded city-bred, sophisticated. "No. Destroy it completely. Regnault doesn't want to leave anything to chance that might hinder Odo's awakening."

Owyn ventured closer, peering around the curve of a pillar. Two men in black robes stood in the center of a breach in a ten-foot-high wall of stones. Their hoods were down and sweat rolled down their faces. Each gripped a large maul and the floor around them was littered with chunks of debris. A glowing iron brazier stood close by, its bowl filled with burning cords of wood.

Beyond the breach in the wall was what looked like a large, square, stone door with matching handles on each side but no apparent hinge. He realized the wall must have concealed the door before the cultists battered it down. Owyn could make out runes, some of which he recognized as symbols of protection, carved into the stones of the two sections of wall which still stood.

The men hefted their mauls and resumed their destruction.

Owyn looked down the row of columns to his left, then to his right. He knew he couldn't stay there, but he had no inkling of which way he should go. Then he spotted a bobbing light, approaching from farther down the colonnade, and that decided it for him.

He darted toward the left-hand side of the vault, away from the light, praying the rhythmic pounding of the cultists' mauls would cover the sound of his footsteps.

The two men paused in their labor just as Owyn's boot struck a pile of shattered granite he'd failed to notice in the darkness, and the shards clattered across the stone floor. He winced, rooted to the spot, holding his breath and hoping the interposing columns and the ringing echoes would cause the men to disregard the noise.

"What was that?" one of the men said, picking up a torch and igniting it in the brazier.

Owyn broke into a run. Both men gave chase.

He sprinted down the colonnade, their labored breaths and rustling robes at his back. Their torchlight threw his shadow ahead of him, elongated and twisted.

Just as he neared the wall of the vault, Owyn spared a backward glance. He was outpacing his pursuers, but they did not appear to be giving up.

Still looking over his shoulder, Owyn collided with something strong and springy. The left side of his body was plastered to something like a giant spider-web.

The two men slowed their pace and approached, wearing confused expressions that quickly transformed into sadistic glee.

Their celebration was cut short as something dropped from the ceiling. It landed atop one of the men and bore him to the ground, simultaneously sending the other man sprawling. The torch fell from the second man's hand and rolled toward Owyn, sputtering as it traveled across the floor. It came to rest about five yards away, threatening to go out.

Owyn looked on in horror at the thing on top of the cultist. It was a spider the size of a mastiff, bristling with short, wiry hair. Its eyes, shimmering in the guttering torchlight like a pair of thousand-faceted rubies, bulged out of its head above a wicked set of razor-sharp mandibles. He watched as it leaped from its first victim to the second, who was just scrambling to his feet, and it clung to the man's chest as he was knocked down once more.

Owyn saw the spider's head dip and watched the mandibles close around the cultist's shoulder, piercing flesh and bone. He grimaced as the man let out an agonized scream.

Finally, the man stopped screaming, but Owyn could hear him panting heavily. He looked back toward the first man then. His eyes were open, but he did not move save for the shallow rise and fall of his chest.

As Owyn struggled to free himself, he realized he was caught in a giant web stretched out between the pillars on either side of the exit. Try as he might, he found it impossible to move anything touching the web. His left arm and leg were completely trapped.

He pulled his dagger with his right hand and began to saw at one of the web strands.

Owyn shot a nervous glance toward the spider just as it sidled back toward the first cultist. His heart was hammering in his chest and pulsing in his throat.

Dread washed over him as he realized just how little progress his dagger was making on the thick web strand. He didn't have much time before the spider decided to come for him.

Staring at the faltering torch, Owyn sheathed his dagger and pulled at the pack on his back. To his dismay, he found that it, too, was stuck fast to the web. Desperate, he drew the dagger again and stabbed it into the bottom of his pack. It was an awkward angle, working with the blade behind his back, but he carefully cut an opening big enough for the object he wanted.

His tinderbox spilled out and rattled onto the ground before he could stop it. Owyn sheathed the dagger and reached into the hole in his pack. He looked back toward the spider in time to see it bite into the already unconscious cultist.

It seemed to dance on its long hairy legs as it turned to face him.

Owyn found what he was looking for and carefully withdrew it from his pack. A small clay jar with a cork, sealed with wax. He aimed it carefully as the spider prowled toward him with an unsettling gait. Throwing it as best he could from his current position, the jar hit the spider just off center of its thorax, but it bounced from its carapace and broke open on the ground in front of it.

The spider's mandibles clicked in agitation, but it was undeterred by the puddle of spilled oil, scuttling directly through the substance in a straight line toward Owyn just as swiftly as before.

He reached quickly back into the hole in his pack. He had one more chance. The spider had reached the place where the flickering torch lay and was just beginning to sidle around it when Owyn managed to liberate the last jar of oil from his pack.

This time he did not aim for the spider, at least not directly. He cast the jar horizontally as if he were skipping a stone across a pond. The jar hit the floor with a glancing impact, a foot in front of the torch, where it shattered and sent a spray of oil flying toward both the torch and the creature. There was a flash and then the spider was engulfed. It skittered away from Owyn in a panicked retreat which only served to further stoke the flames on its hairy body. It raced up a column toward the ceiling before suddenly falling back toward the ground, landing on its back with a sickening thud. As the flames sputtered out, the spider pulled its legs into itself and ceased to move. The repellent stench from the thing's smoking carcass made Owyn's eyes water.

A distant light drew his attention then. A flickering torch, presumably the light he had seen earlier, approaching from the far side of the vault. Owyn closed his eyes and pretended to be unconscious. He could hear the tread of boots now, drawing near.

"Cadoc? Lewyn! Bloody hells! What's this then?" An unfamiliar voice.

The footsteps came closer, and the inside of Owyn's eyelids grew red as he felt the heat from the torch near his face. He held his breath and concentrated on holding every muscle in his body still, except for his right hand, which closed around the hilt of his dagger.

In a blur, Owyn plunged the dagger into the man's neck.

The cultist staggered backward, and Owyn turned the dagger loose, reaching out to snatch the torch from the man's hand.

While the man gurgled incoherently on the ground, Owyn held the torch overhead and touched it to the web, moving it slowly in an arc. Acrid, black smoke issued from the web. In seconds, he was free.

The cultist grew quiet, and Owyn stared down, filled with disgust. He had killed him.

Owyn was loath to touch him, but he needed his dagger back.

The boy knelt and clenched his teeth as he gripped the dagger. He tugged. The dead man's head jerked toward him, but the dagger was still lodged in place. He pulled harder. There was a squelch and then the resistance was gone. The blade slipped from the wound with ease and Owyn retched.

After the nausea passed, Owyn looked at each of the other two men. Foam flecked their lips. Their chests barely moved.

He knew it was reckless not to finish them off, but he couldn't bring himself to take their lives while they were helpless.

He turned and hurried through the exit and into another long passageway.

CHAPTER SIX

Owyn found himself in darkness again, his torch having gone out.

He was hungry and thirsty. He couldn't do anything about his hunger, but his leather flask still had water in it. He took a drink.

Removing his pack, Owyn felt inside, finding only the hole he'd slashed in the bottom. All his gear was gone, except for the flask around his neck and the sword and dagger at his waist.

He tossed the ruined pack aside, frustration and helplessness rising in him. Tears welled in his eyes, but he thought of Bledig and held them back.

Bledig was most likely dead, but the thought of his master lingering as a spirit in this cursed place, watching him, forged a new sense of determination in the boy. If Bledig could see him somehow, he didn't want the old Silverman to see him cry. He wanted to make him proud, at least once. That thought steadied his hands. He got moving.

He had only gone a few steps, feeling his way along, when he discovered a slight divot in the wall. It was subtle, likely to have been missed by torchlight, but the careful probing of his hands had caught it. Owyn slid two fingers into the hollow until they touched a small knot, distinct from the surrounding stone. He pressed it, and it sank into the wall.

A puff of cooler air touched his cheeks, and he sensed the movement as a section of the wall swung inward.

Grimacing, he entered the concealed passage. His outstretched hand found the edge of the false wall, and he closed it carefully behind him.

He started forward and nearly tumbled down a flight of steps that dropped steeply just inside the secret door. Collecting himself, he descended backward, crawling on all fours and carefully probing each step with his boot.

Owyn counted thirteen steps before he reached a dead end. Turning around, he examined the stones with his hands.

Just as he was about to give up, his fingers touched an iron lever. He pulled it and heard a section of the wall swing away from him.

Owyn ducked through the opening, leaving this panel open behind him. He moved cautiously, keeping his hands out before him until they encountered what seemed to be an upright, iron sarcophagus. His fingers traced a raised, stylized figure embossed on the front, bisected vertically by a seam.

Backing away from the strangely designed sarcophagus, he ran into another piece of furniture and reached back with a sharp intake of breath, his hands pricked by multiple needlepoints.

Gingerly, he investigated and found that it was a table, embedded with nails, the points sticking toward the ceiling.

He turned, and his knee collided with something hard and immovable.

Owyn sat down, clutching his knee. Blood seeped through a new hole in his breeches.

Once the initial pain subsided, Owyn examined the device that had tripped him. It was an iron chair, secured to the floor with iron bolts. It had large, flat-topped arm rests topped with leather straps and buckles.

His skin prickled with dawning horror. He had read about implements such as this in his studies. He was in a torture chamber!

Owyn wanted out, immediately. He crawled as swiftly as he dared, trying to avoid any other grisly devices lurking in the darkness, until he reached a wooden cabinet of some sort.

Using it for support, he rose to his feet and found that the cabinet had a countertop at about chest height. He searched the countertop in the darkness and found several metal implements, some clearly knives, and others more curiously fashioned. There were also several glass jars and bottles, all empty.

He grinned mirthlessly when his fingers found a candle next to a tinderbox.

Moments later, a dim flame bobbed atop a candle made of motley-colored wax.

Owyn turned slowly and examined what he could of the room in the weak candlelight. As he'd suspected, it was filled with various torture devices. A surge of revulsion rose in him as he imagined the doomed souls who had met an agonizing fate there, all for the pleasure of a depraved lord.

To his left, at the end of the room opposite the secret door he had entered, was the real door to the room, wooden and banded with iron. Cobwebs hung from the corners of the ceiling as well as many of the devices.

Owyn turned back toward the cabinet, intent on finding anything else that might be useful. As he did so, he saw the relief of a large, demonic face, high on the wall near the ceiling. He shivered, and started to look away, but something about the eyes demanded his attention.

He walked toward the face and stood beneath it. The eyes were carved in such a way that they formed two narrow holes, each angled downward toward the room below. *Strange*, he thought. If someone were to lie prone in the passage beyond the wall, they might look down into the chamber.

A hollow, reverberating voice suddenly sounded from the face, and Owyn held his breath, certain it had come to life, intent on dragging him to hell.

"What is this?" it said.

"It's a backpack," said another voice, with a refined accent. "It doesn't look old, either. There is a hole in the bottom, but this can't have been here for decades."

"Keep your eyes sharp. According to the map, there are steps leading to a chamber just around this corner."

Owyn blew out the candle hastily, plunging himself back into total darkness, heart pounding, paralyzed with uncertainty, yet certain enemies would soon be upon him.

As he stood there, indecisive, a yellow glow entered the demon's right eye and then its left, just for a moment, and then they were dark again. Owyn jolted into action. He grabbed the contents of the tinderbox in the darkness and quickly retraced his steps back to the secret door. He closed it behind him just as the wooden door on the opposite end of the room opened.

He scrambled up the steep steps, slipped through the second secret door, and cautiously peered into the passageway. It was dark, and as far as he could discern, deserted.

He crept forward until he found two pinholes of light, close together, near the floor. Getting down on his belly, Owyn put his eyes to the holes and found that he was looking down into the room he had just vacated. It was now well lit with torches. Five men in black robes strode across the room. One carried a body over his shoulder.

Another, the hem of his black robe embroidered with gold, spoke to the others in an authoritative tone. "Someone has been here recently. Probably the owner of the pack we just found. No matter. Place him there."

The cultist carrying the body dropped it roughly onto the table with the nailbed atop it. The victim moaned and lifted his gray-haired head slightly.

Owyn stifled a gasp.

Bledig! He was still alive!

Another cultist handed Bledig's pack to the one with the embroidered robe, who then upended it, dumping out all the contents. A copper kettle hummed as it hit the stone floor amid several scattered pouches.

The leader had a low forehead, black hair, and a thin straight nose. He grabbed Bledig roughly by the chin. "Who sent you?"

"What have you done with the boy?" Bledig rasped.

"Nothing yet. Who sent you?" he demanded.

"No one sent me. Don't hurt the boy. He isn't—" A violent fit of coughing cut the Silverman's words short.

The cultist leaned down toward his captive. "We'll do with him as we please, but I promise you it will be far worse for him if you do not answer my questions. Why are you here?"

Bledig's voice was hoarse. "I am from Caer Argyn."

"Galani Yidwyr? *Silvermen*, here?" the leader spat in denial.

"I am," Bledig croaked, "but the boy is only a fledgling in my care. He is of no consequence to you or anyone else."

The cultist scoffed.

Bledig suddenly seemed more alert. "I recognize that brand on your wrist. You're a member of the stonemason's guild."

The man sneered. "Not a member—I'm the *guildmaster* of Thiardun's stonemason's guild."

"Regnault," another cultist warned.

The guildmaster shot a baleful glare at the man who had spoken.

Bledig glanced from the other cultists back to Regnault. "What demonic designs have brought you to this ghost-haunted place?"

Regnault paced a few steps away, then faced Bledig again. "My master has commanded me to rouse one of his faithful disciples."

Bledig's confused expression evolved into disbelief. "You can't mean Odo," he said. "You don't know what you are saying. You would unleash a plague of bloodshed and suffering!"

"A temple cannot rise without shaping the stones to build it," Regnault replied coolly, his gaze flicking over Bledig. "The serfs of this land are no more than that—raw material to be shaped and used to build an eternal legacy."

The disbelief faded from Bledig's face. "I see. This thing you serve has promised you something. No demonic promises could justify this. Don't you already have enough wealth and power?"

Regnault gestured impatiently. "There is no such thing as enough. Not of wealth. Not of power. But once I complete this task, my master will grant me a great deal more of both. Come, you can greet Odo yourself. Once he has fed upon the pretty morsel we've brought him, perhaps he'll still be hungry." He snapped his fingers. "Bring him!"

Two of the cultists lifted Bledig from the table. He winced, blood trickling from his mouth and a score of wounds on his back.

As they made their way to the door they had used to enter the chamber, Owyn tore himself away from his vantage point and scurried back to the secret entrance to the stairs.

This time, he hurried down the stone steps in the darkness, heedless of the danger, and back through the second secret door.

Owyn reached the demon face just as a yellow glow passed from its left eye to its right, then vanished. They'd gone back the way they'd come.

He stood in the darkness, fists clenched, breath tight in his throat.

Bledig was alive. But Owyn had no idea how to save him or what to do next.

He was trapped in a nightmare from which he could not wake. But if Bledig still fought, so would he.

CHAPTER SEVEN

Owyn stared at the contents from Bledig's pack, scattered across the floor.

Stooping, he began gathering the items and placing them back inside. It was pointless, maybe, but they were Bledig's things, and he couldn't bring himself to leave them strewn across the floor.

Dread twisted in his gut. He recalled Regnault's words about waking Odo. About feeding Bledig—and someone else—to the thing.

There were at least five cultists who had Bledig. Possibly more. How could he hope to prevail against such overwhelming odds?

As he worked, two small pouches caught his eye—the Aylruna and Wyrmwort.

Only yesterday, they'd sat comfortably in a warm tavern. Bledig had berated him for confusing the herb that bolstered courage with the one that drew the dead. It had stung then. Now, Owyn would give anything to hear one of Bledig's scoldings.

He smiled faintly. For all his lessons, no root or rune in his master's bag could stop living men with blades.

The smile faded. He lingered, staring at the two pouches.

Then he gently tossed one in the air and caught it.

Slipping the other into the pack, he stood and crossed to the cabinet along the wall. He poured the last of the water from his flask into Bledig's copper kettle, filling it nearly to the brim.

He tipped the pouch's contents into the kettle, then held it over the candle-flame and said a silent prayer.

CHAPTER EIGHT

Bledig grimaced as he was tossed unceremoniously onto the rubble-strewn ground beside another figure.

He turned and saw a girl with fair hair, only a little older than Owyn. She lay on her belly, wrists tied behind her, her ankles bound. Her dress was torn and dirt-smeared, her tear-streaked face hollow with fear.

Recognition flickered across the Silverman's face. "You were at the tavern yesterday."

The girl nodded, drawing a trembling breath. "After everyone ran out, two men grabbed me. Took me out back. There were more waiting in the forest." She stifled a sob. "Martin said he would look after me, but..."

A boot slammed into Bledig's ribs, making him grunt as he drew his knees slightly toward his chest.

"Shut your mouths," barked a robed fanatic, looming over him.

Through slitted eyes, Bledig watched as the rest of the men clustered around a sealed portal ahead. It was a massive square slab of stone, six feet on each side, with no visible hinge and an iron handle inset on each side.

"You. Grab that handle. And you, grab the other," Regnault ordered.

Two of the cultists hesitated, then obeyed. Regnault made a circling gesture. Each man turned his handle.

A hiss issued from the edges of the slab as something deep within it unlocked, followed by a wave of fetid air that rolled over them.

"The rest of you—push."

All except Regnault pressed against the stone. Slowly, the slab began to slide inward like a great plug on hidden rails. The guildmaster followed behind, torch in hand, as they pushed it thirty feet or more into a tunnel beyond.

Bledig looked to the girl beside him. "I don't know what they plan for us. But stay strong. Say a prayer, if you've a mind to. Whatever comes, it'll be over soon."

The girl's face tightened. She nodded, swallowing her fear.

Three of the men returned. One hauled the girl to her feet, and the two others seized Bledig. They dragged them down the narrow passage.

At the far end, one of the cultists reached into a wall recess and flipped a heavy iron lever.

There was a deep mechanical click from inside the slab, but nothing moved.

"Lift it!" Regnault ordered.

The men scrambled to grip the handles. Grunting with effort, they raised the slab. Inch by trembling inch, the great stone rose vertically toward the ceiling until it hovered overhead.

"Secure it," Regnault growled.

Two cultists produced tools and thick wedges from their packs. They shoved the blocks into place beneath the slab. Using mallets, they hammered in long iron spikes beneath the blocks to brace them.

"Are you sure those'll hold?" one muttered. "The portal only opens from this side."

"Of course it does," Regnault snapped. "And yes, they will hold. Bring them."

More torches were lit, smoke and heat mingling with the stale breath of whatever lay ahead.

As they were hauled forward past the threshold, Bledig's pulse quickened. The girl gasped beside him.

He looked at her. Despite the ache in his ribs and the growing fear in his chest, he gave her the faintest smile.

"Courage," he said.

CHAPTER NINE

Owyn retraced his path to the spider's remains, the lingering stench of burnt hair and charred meat guiding him forward like a foul, unseen landmark through the dark. He'd extinguished his candle before entering the vault.

He passed the three bodies, reached the intersection where the two rows of columns met, and turned left.

He had to go very slowly as he made his way across the rubble from the demolished wall. The enormous stone block which had previously resided in the center of the wall was gone, leaving behind a black void.

His eyes gradually discerned a passage beyond the void which ran a straight course for many yards before connecting with another chamber of unknown size. The exit at the other end of the passage was framed by the glow of distant torches.

Owyn crept forward quietly, his leather flask in his left hand. As he entered the passage, he noted there were a pair of deep grooves in the floor, spaced roughly three feet apart, which ran parallel down the center.

He pressed on and heard several voices chanting in the distance. The air felt heavy and malevolent, reeking of tomb dust and rot.

The grooves in the floor ended along with the passage, and there was a maul leaning against each side. He looked up at the stone slab that had once sealed the passage, now precariously held in place above his head by wooden blocks and iron spikes.

At the bottom of the slab, two stone protrusions matched the size and position of the grooves in the floor. There was a shallow alcove to his left.

Owyn crouched in the dark and peered into the enormous vault ahead.

Supporting a ceiling lost in gloom, a double row of thick stone columns stretched away from him toward the far end of the vault, where a giant black idol loomed some fifty yards distant.

A broad raised platform squatted in the center of the vault, wide steps leading up on all sides. Atop the platform, near the edge closest to Owyn, sat an altar cut from a single chunk of onyx. A prone figure struggled atop the altar, and beyond it, the cultists were gathered around a basalt sarcophagus.

Owyn counted six of them. Each held a blazing torch, their free hands held high in exultation. He looked back at the figure upon the altar and realized it was a girl.

There was no sign of Bledig.

Owyn needed to get closer. He looked for the best route toward the platform and noticed several other sarcophagi arranged around its base, between the columns and the steps.

He slunk to the first column on his left.

His heart was racing. He gave himself just a moment to be sure he was in control of his breathing so that he wouldn't give himself away.

Then he was on the move again.

He padded from column to column, heart hammering, muscles taut. Shadows clung to the stone, but he kept watch on the cultists' shifting gazes, timing his moves between their glances.

The girl on the altar tugged futilely at the ropes binding her. He could see her more clearly now, and a jolt of recognition stopped him cold. It was Briann. The girl from the tavern.

"Why is he not rising?" one of the cultists asked, interrupting the chant. "Perhaps we are not speaking the words correctly."

Owyn froze. He had been about to dart toward the next column when the impatient cultist's query had caused the leader to turn.

"Be quiet!" Regnault snarled. "He will rise, damn you. He has been entombed for a hundred years. We just need to give him some incentive." He strode quickly toward the altar with a dagger in his hand, grabbed hold of one of Briann's ankles, and straightened her leg. Then he drew the edge of the blade along the outside of her thigh, and she screamed.

Bledig suddenly appeared, rising awkwardly, from the far side of the altar, his hands bound behind his back.

"Don't touch her!" he shouted.

Regnault backhanded him. Bledig toppled over, landing hard at the top of the left-hand flight of steps.

Owyn's instinct was to run to Bledig and the girl, but he resisted, knowing it would spell disaster for all of them.

He stayed motionless instead. He needed to be sure the fanatics were focused on the opposite direction.

As he waited, an otherworldly murmur reached Owyn's ears. The hair on his neck and arms stood on end. He glanced at the cultists to confirm the sound wasn't coming from them but they seemed just as startled.

They turned toward the idol and Owyn followed their gaze. It was a monstrosity carved from the same black onyx as the altar—obscene in both shape and scale. Its belly was bloated and corpulent, and its grotesquely elongated head was wrong in every way, with thick, froglike lips stretched across the top of its face and, below them, a cluster of jade eyes gleaming coldly. Bull-like horns jutted from its skull, and great bat wings rose from its back. Its legs ended in cloven hooves, and each of its hands ended in eight long, clawed fingers.

It was Regnault who broke the silence first. "Oh, great and terrible Molzu'uk," he intoned. "Grant us your accursed favor from the voids beyond reality and the shattered illusions of time. Awaken your disciple, so that he might serve you according to your will."

The other cultists echoed the words in unison, their voices rising in unholy harmony.

It was now or never. Owyn held his breath, and he advanced to the next column. Taking cover behind the column, he was now even with the corner of the platform.

The chanting from the cultists changed. It was now an unfamiliar tongue that sounded old and sinister.

Owyn lowered himself flat and crawled on all fours to the bottom of the steps.

Taking several slow breaths, he waited to be sure he hadn't been seen. The fanatics' liturgy swelled into a wild, impassioned frenzy.

He crawled up the steps to where Bledig lay. A flicker of surprise—and something harder to read—passed over the Silverman's face when he saw Owyn.

The boy brought his finger to his lips and drew his dagger. Bledig shook his head and mouthed the word, "Go."

Owyn ignored him, sat his flask down, and began to saw through his mentor's bonds, glancing nervously between the cultists and his handiwork. Their attention was still completely fixed on the idol.

Having freed Bledig's hands, Owyn quickly cut through the bonds at his ankles.

Finished, he was about to edge to the altar when suddenly the chanting ceased with a collective gasp from the zealots.

Owyn heard stone scraping against stone, echoing throughout the vault. It came from all around the bottom of the platform as well as the top.

He looked around frantically and saw the lids of the sarcophagi all slowly pushed to the side.

"Yes! Yes! I told you he would rise!" Regnault shouted in exultation.

Owyn picked up his flask and stood behind the altar. Briann turned her head toward him, eyes filled with fear, but then they locked with his and he saw recognition in them. He held his finger to his lips, and she nodded. Then he began to cut hurriedly through the rope binding her wrists.

There was a clamor of stone lids clattering against the floor all around, adding to the echoes reverberating in the chamber.

Owyn looked past the cultists and saw an emaciated, corpselike creature sit up in the sarcophagus. The leathery skin on its face was remarkably intact, but its eyes were empty hollows. It stretched its clawlike hands out to the sides of the sarcophagus and pulled itself upright. It placed a foot tentatively atop the platform. Then another. Treading unsteadily as if it were blind.

"Yes, Lord Odo!" Regnault fawned. "We have freed you and brought you something to restore yourself. Look here!" He pivoted then, and his face turned livid when he saw Owyn lifting the girl from the altar and setting her on her feet.

Six more walking corpses with empty eye sockets stepped uncertainly from their sarcophagi, three on each side of the platform, and began stiffly ascending the steps.

"Take them!" Regnault screamed to the other men. "They can feed on all three of them!" The cultists drew daggers and scimitars as they took a step toward Owyn and the girl. Bledig grasped the altar and pulled himself to his feet with a grimace.

"Wait!" Owyn shouted, holding the flask out in front of himself.

The cultists paused, perhaps confused by the absurdity of being threatened with a water flask. They looked to their leader for guidance.

The walking corpses had reached the top of the platform. Odo stood close behind Regnault.

"What are you doing?" Bledig rasped at Owyn. "Take the girl and run!"

Ignoring his mentor, Owyn tossed the flask high into the air. The fanatics watched it fall as the boy drew his sword and cleaved the flask with one smooth stroke.

The clear fluid flecked with tiny bits of red and yellow matter sprayed outward in an arc, drenching the dumbfounded zealots. They flinched, as if they were expecting the liquid to be acid or some other harmful agent.

Nothing happened.

Full of indignation, Regnault wiped his face dry with the sleeve of his robe. "I will enjoy watching Odo drain the life from your worthless hide." He moved aside so that Odo could pass. "Take the miserable whelp first."

Instead of advancing toward Owyn, however, the thing that was Odo wrapped its deathlike hands around Regnault's throat. The guildmaster's flesh glowed with a ghastly witchlight around the creature's clawlike fingers.

“No!” Regnault cried out. “What are you doing? It is I who freed—” His outrage was cut short as his words broke into a rasping cough. His skin shriveled, drying as if every drop of moisture were being sucked away. Then came a brittle crack, and his withered husk crumpled to the floor.

The other cultists gaped at their fallen leader in horror. Only for an instant—then each had a corpse’s hands wrapped around their own throats.

Owyn snatched up a guttering torch dropped by one of the cultists. “Now we run!” he shouted. “Go!”

He gave the girl a slight shove, then pulled Bledig’s arm around his neck and helped him down the steps. The three fled the chamber without looking back.

In the passage, Bledig leaned against the wall near the recess and shoved the lever upward. The slab groaned but did not move.

Owyn handed the torch to Briann, grabbed a maul, and swung at the iron spikes. The maul was awkward in his hands, too heavy to be swung effectively.

He dropped it, drew his sword, and began chopping at one of the wooden blocks. He chipped away until it splintered, and the slab dropped half an inch, dislodging a spike.

“Help him out of here,” he said to Briann.

She nodded and supported Bledig by the arm as they hobbled down the passage.

Owyn turned to the remaining block and hacked at it with frantic strokes.

The walking corpses had descended the steps and were advancing steadily toward him. Baleful orbs of green eldritch fire now burned in their eye sockets. Before, they had seemed blind—now they were watching. Their withered arms were stretched out before them, and an echoing susurrus was building, rising in both volume and intensity.

With a final cry, Owyn smote the remnants of the block with all his strength. The wood flew apart. The slab dropped to the floor with a thunderous boom, sending a shower of iron spikes clattering in its wake.

Owyn placed his palm on the slab.

It lurched toward him.

He turned and ran. The slab thundered after him, hurtling through the tunnel as if loosed by the fury of the cultists' dark god.

He leaped from the passage just as the portal sealed with a shuddering rumble of grinding stone. The two iron handles spun around once with an audible click.

Breathing heavily, hand to his forehead, Owyn turned to face his companions.

Briann stood at the intersection of columns, holding the torch. She gave Owyn an exhausted smile, relief and disbelief mingled in her expression.

Bledig sagged against a pillar.

Owyn rushed to his side. "Are you all right?" he asked, brow furrowed.

Bledig placed his hand on Owyn's shoulder for support. "I'll live, but I'll need some stitches and herbs."

The Silverman started to stagger alongside him, but pulled back, leaning against the pillar and studying Owyn with a strange look in his eye.

"What is it?" the boy asked, trying to read his master's expression.

"Aylruna?" Bledig asked, lifting an eyebrow.

"Aylruna," Owyn said, smiling as he realized what that look in Bledig's eye meant. Admiration. "Draws the dead like flies to honey."

The Silverman smiled back. "I underestimated you, boy. You'll make a Silverman after all."

A SOLDIER'S LAMENT

CHAPTER ONE

Garrett approached the gatehouse of Thiardun's outer wall on horseback. Orange flames danced above the iron brazier beyond the portcullis. It was the smallest of the city's eastern gates, and the only one this side of the river still operational after dark, given that it faced toward the border with Besh and away from the more civilized territories of the kingdom proper. Inside, armed guards stood silhouetted against the firelight.

The odds of anyone here knowing him were slim. He only hoped they wouldn't ask questions about where he'd come from or where he was headed. He was too exhausted for lies.

Garrett frowned, glancing down at his boots and breeches, stained with mud and... something darker. He wore no armor, having abandoned it when he deserted the baron's army.

His growling stomach was louder to him than the clatter of his stolen horse's hooves as he brought the animal to a halt before the gate. Dismounting, he gave a false name to the guards. They were an uninquisitive pair; though they looked him up and down, neither asked what business he had in the city.

The postern creaked open beside the sealed portcullis. The guards watched in silence as he passed.

He pressed the fold of his cloak against his longsword to conceal it. After the battle at High Valley and the carnage that followed, he'd sworn to himself there would be no more killing. Despite this, the sword still hung from his belt. He'd worn it comfortably for more than a decade in service to the crown, but now it chafed against his thigh.

The first thing Garrett intended to do in the morning was trade the weapon for whatever silver he could and buy new clothes. The second thing would be to get back on the road. He needed to find a refuge that didn't have any use for soldiers. Somewhere he could learn an honest trade, even find work on a farm. Hell, he'd do anything that didn't require a sword.

With the light from the brazier behind him, he led the horse down a street illuminated only by the gibbous moon and the occasional glimmer between loose-fitting shutters.

Garrett just needed to lie low in Thiardun for the night without calling any attention to himself. After provisioning in the morning, he would head west, into the heart of the kingdom, and get far away from the troubled frontier of Besh.

The street stank of piss and other foulness. Sidestepping a puddle of slime, Garrett caught a glimpse of movement across the street and looked up to see a figure following another toward an alley.

A tall man with a well-trimmed beard staggered forward, a broad, drunken smile on his face. He wore a green silk doublet and hose—far too elegant for the poorest district in the city.

The woman wore a thick red hooded cloak. The details of her face were hidden. Only her luminous eyes shone out from beneath the hood as she turned back toward her suitor and crooked a finger at him. She disappeared into the mouth of the alley and a light feminine giggle echoed from within. The laughter spurred the man onward, and soon he too was lost in the shadows of the alley.

Cheapside, as all the locals called the Tradesward, had an entire street devoted to brothels—the Whisper Walk, if he remembered correctly. But it didn't surprise Garrett to see a harlot plying her trade in the filthy streets. After all, he had made his way to the low quarter intentionally. His reserve of silver was alarmingly small, and he knew the more elegant areas of the city were well beyond his means.

Garrett passed the entrance to the alley the couple had entered. His horse whickered nervously and jerked to a sudden stop, the muscles in her flanks quivering.

"Easy." Gently stroking her muzzle, he coaxed her forward.

They continued for a few blocks before Garrett paused and brought the horse to a halt. He listened for any telltale sound of an inn or tavern that might still be open, but the night was silent.

His shoulders slumped with weariness. He tugged at the horse's reins, and they pressed on, hooves echoing through the narrow, empty streets.

CHAPTER TWO

Before long, they approached a squat, single-story building. Without warning, the horse reversed and began to pull at the reins.

"What's gotten into you?" Garrett tugged the reins in the opposite direction. The horse stopped but let out a loud snort of protest.

His expression puzzled, Garrett looked down and noticed dark stains in the gutter. Then he noticed the sweet, metallic scent. His chest tightened.

He looked around in alarm, then his eyes followed the dark trail. The building appeared to be where the blood stains had originated. Above the recessed doorway of the building hung a wooden sign. Barely visible in the wan moonlight, it depicted a lamb and cleaver.

"Gods, I'm just as skittish as you." He tried to force a chuckle at himself but found that he was unable.

"Spare a coin, sir," came a woman's hungry, husky voice from the shadowed door stoop of the butcher shop, startling him.

Without stirring the shadows, the owner of the voice stepped forward—a middle-aged woman in a peasant dress with long, unkempt brown hair. In her arms she held a small, swaddled form.

Garrett let out a long, slow breath, relieved at the sight of her. For a moment, he'd held it, anticipating something dangerous. "My lady, this is not a place for such as yourself to be after dark."

She scoffed. "It's not by choice, I assure you. I have hearth and home, but there's nothing in the cupboards for these little ones."

Two small children, a boy and a girl, came forward from the shadows. Neither stood taller than their mother's waist. They pressed against her and clung to her dress.

At the sight of the children, another image came into Garrett's mind, unbidden, and he blinked to disperse the tears that formed.

He cleared his throat and sniffed, doing his best to regain his composure. Taking his coin purse from his belt, he sighed.

"I don't have much to give. Barely enough for a meal tonight, if I'm being honest. But you're welcome to a third of what little I have." He shook a single silver coin into his palm and held it out to them.

The woman's eyes brightened, but the children shrank back behind her. "Bless you for your generosity, sir. But why don't we help each other? You can spend the night under our roof instead of paying for an inn, and I'll use that to buy something to cook for you come morning."

Garrett gave the woman a sorrowful smile. He couldn't bear the thought of being under the same roof as the children—not after what he'd seen in that village.

"That is a fine offer, madam, but I sadly must decline. The silver is still yours, however."

She frowned. Holding her swaddled bundle against her breast with one arm, she walked toward him and held out a hand adorned with a fingerless wool mitten.

Garrett placed the silver regal into her palm.

"Thank you," she said, somewhat stiffly.

Afraid that he had somehow insulted her by refusing her invitation, Garrett responded, "I could greatly use your assistance with some directions. Where *is* the closest inn?"

"It's not far. Keep going until you reach the river. Then turn right and stop before you reach Sinners Alley. You'll hear it. The Dancing Pig. The patrons aren't as polite as yourself, but it's about the best you'll find at this hour in Cheapside."

Garrett bowed his head at her. She returned the gesture.

He had to pull fiercely at his horse's reins before it would move, and then they were on their way once more.

CHAPTER THREE

Garrett handed off his horse and another precious silver regal to the stableboy, then circled to the front of the inn. He couldn't afford a room, but a bowl of warm food would be enough. He'd sneak back later and sleep in the stall with his horse.

Climbing the wooden steps to the door, Garrett glanced at the crudely painted sign overhead, a pig standing on its hind legs, before entering.

The common room was just as shabby as he'd expected, dimly lit by oil lamps and a lone fireplace, with a low ceiling and a press of rough-looking men in sweat-stained tunics and filthy gambesons. Some hunched over tables, others leaned belly-up to an oak bar that hadn't seen polish in years. Behind it stood a thick-jowled barkeep in a grease-streaked leather apron, watching the room with dull eyes.

Garrett swept the room with a glance, avoiding eye contact as best he could. Instinct and experience told him this was a dangerous place, even for killers—let alone a deserter on the run, with a shaky sword arm and a hole in his memory. But he planned to keep to himself and steer clear of trouble.

The volume of voices shouting and laughing negated any thought of a quiet meal, but for Garrett the less opportunity for self-reflection the better.

He waited for an opening at the bar and placed his last coin down on its coarse wooden surface.

"Ain't seen you in 'ere before," the barkeep said. "Travel far, 'ave ya?"

Keeping his head down, Garrett replied, "Not yet, but I'm headed out east with a caravan to re-supply the army." It was the best he could think of.

"That so?" said the barkeep. "You look like a man who's marched a few leagues. You army yerself?"

Garrett scoffed nervously. "Me? My old pap—Millenoth rest him—would laugh himself sick at that." He tapped the coin with his index finger. "Is that enough for a drink and some grub?"

The barkeep rubbed his stubbly jowls, eyeing Garrett suspiciously.

A moment later, burdened with a flagon of ale and a bowl of stew, Garrett made his way to a small, unoccupied table against the wall. He sat down with his back toward the door and his right flank exposed to the room. He hoped to go unnoticed by anyone who might give him problems. He just wanted to fill his belly and then slink off to the stable until dawn.

As he chewed a bland chunk of gristle, Garrett noticed a small-framed woman with sable hair that fell midway down her back. Although he kept his head down, he couldn't help but follow her in the corner of his eye.

The woman's red dress dragged the floor as she sauntered across the room toward the bar, then leaned in toward the barkeep and appeared to whisper something into his ear.

Garrett resisted the urge to look at her directly, but he could see that she was now leaning with her back against the bar, elbows casually draped over its top. He had the odd feeling that she was looking right at him.

She straightened and began to walk toward him, a slow sensuousness about her movements.

Midway across the room, the woman passed a crowded table and caught the eye of a brutish man with receding red hair. His arm shot out and encircled her waist, lifting her from the floor as he stood up, before sitting back down and dropping her onto his lap.

Seated to the brute's left, a pock-faced man with half an ear missing roared with laughter, followed by the other four cutthroats at the table.

"What's the matter, my little concubine?" The brute's manner was lecherous to the point of absurdity, which sent his comrades into a fresh fit of laughter.

Garrett turned his head slightly so that he could see the woman's face. Her cheeks were hollow, just shy of gaunt, lending her features an undeniably exotic quality. Her lips were full, her skin like alabaster, and she had large, luminous eyes the color of citrine. She was staring straight at him.

She turned to face the ruffian upon whose lap she sat. Her manner was self-assured as if, despite appearances, she was the one in control. “You would be wise to remove your hands.”

Garrett could not place her accent, but it hinted of the Blistering Lands of the far south.

In response, the red-haired brute grabbed her shoulders and shook them back and forth, but the act was only playful on the surface. It was clearly meant to demean and humiliate her.

Garrett stared into his bowl.

A voice in his head whispered, *Aren't you going to defend me?*

His jaws clenched until he thought his teeth would crack. He couldn't afford to lose control again. Not here.

The woman spoke again. She still seemed aloof to the danger she was in. “Let me go. I won't warn you a third time.”

At this, the bullish thug stopped jostling her and removed his hands. A queer tension stretched between the occupants of the table as they sat silent and immobile, looking toward their leader.

Half-an-ear guffawed suddenly. It sounded unconvincing, but it was enough to break the spell over them. The whole table erupted in hyena laughter and mulelike braying.

Garrett continued to stare into his bowl. The knuckles of the hand that gripped his spoon were turning white.

The brute pivoted the woman on his lap, bringing her nose to his. Any pretense of levity in his words had vanished when he spoke again; there was only cruelty. “Think you're too good for me, whore? Well... I'll teach you your place!”

The other thugs laughed again, but at the brute's expense this time. “She thinks 'erself too good for you, Fergus!”

Fergus's cheeks blushed with rage.

"*Bitch!*" Fergus bellowed, shooting up from his chair and lifting the girl into the air in a single explosion of effort. He roughly pushed her down into a seated position on the edge of the table, overturning several mugs in the process.

Garrett closed his eyes. Images began to swirl behind them. A maelstrom of viscera and violence coalesced into a single tableau of death—one that had haunted his every moment since that last village in Besh.

He told himself again that it wasn't his hands that had done that. *Gods no, not that!* It was the other soldiers who were responsible.

But he couldn't remember everything that had happened there after victory-induced madness had overtaken them. He couldn't be sure what part he'd played in what had happened in that hut.

He heard crude laughter, followed by the sound of tearing fabric, and he remembered where he was. Opening his eyes, he turned toward the spectacle. Fergus was ripping the woman's bodice down the front while his companions held her arms—but her eyes were fixed on Garrett.

Sweat chilled the back of his neck, his heart thudding against his ribs.

"Even a nag can take instruction, if ridden properly," Fergus announced to the room. Several patrons responded with enthusiastic hoots and shouts of encouragement.

Shame brought Garrett unsteadily to his feet. He turned toward the woman and her tormentors.

"That's enough," he heard himself say. His voice sounded weak, uncommitted.

Fergus seemed not to have heard him at all as he continued to tear at her clothing.

Garrett plodded toward them. His hand involuntarily reached for his sword, and it trembled as it touched the hilt.

"I said that's enough," Garrett repeated, this time with a touch more determination.

Fergus spared him a quick glance, which prompted his companions to draw knives, swords, and a hatchet. They began to spread out, creating a circle around Garrett.

"Well, what have we here, lads?" Fergus grinned. "A knight to the rescue? I guess we better *fok* off then, aye?"

One of the thugs rushed Garrett from his right at the same time someone else smashed a clay mug across his left temple. He stumbled forward and a fist slammed into his nose, stunning him.

Hands grabbed him, hoisting him into the air before slamming him down hard enough to split the table beneath him. He landed sprawled across its wreckage, soaked in spilled ale.

Fergus's knee was in his groin, pinning him with his bulk, his fat fist tightening around Garrett's neck. He tried to reach for the dagger sheathed at Fergus's belt, but the brute caught his wrist in a powerful grip with the hand not already around Garrett's throat.

A din of voices swelled around Garrett. In his dimming peripheral vision, he saw the woman leaning against a column, watching him intently with that luminous gaze.

He'd missed her escape amid the sudden eruption of violence. She'd moved too quickly for his eyes to follow, not even leaving a shadow in her wake, and now he'd taken her place.

Garrett knew he was in serious trouble. The hand that wasn't pinned roamed the debris from the table. His fingers happened upon something solid and jagged—a shard from a broken mug. Instinct did the rest.

His hand closed firmly around it, and he drove the shard forcefully into Fergus's neck. Hot crimson sprayed across Garrett's brow, and the brute's hand left his throat to clasp desperately at his own, eyes wide with shock.

The bigger man lurched upright as Garrett pushed himself to his feet. A change had come over the soldier's features—the desperate humanity gone from his expression, it was now cold and detached.

Red gushed between Fergus's fingers as he reached for his dagger.

Garrett ripped his sword free of its scabbard and swept it in a smooth backhanded arc.

Fergus's head flew through the air and struck the bar with a meaty thump.

The common room exploded into chaos. Some patrons ran for the door. Others gaped, open-mouthed. Fergus's companions wasted precious seconds trying to comprehend what had just happened. Before they could recover, Garrett rammed his sword through the torso of one of the thugs before jerking it free and slashing it through the jaw of another. The first man's body hit the floor next to the severed tongue and several teeth from the second.

The next enemy he advanced on had the presence of mind to block with his axe, but Garrett reversed his stroke to cleave the man's wrist, sending the axe and the hand that wielded it tumbling in different directions. He caught the weapon midair and sent it spinning to bury its edge in the chest of another onrushing foe.

Madness took him. He butchered everyone within reach of his blade.

His boots slipped on the gore-slick floor, and he laughed—until he saw what he'd done. The sound caught in his throat. He'd lost himself again.

Bodies and limbs lay scattered across the taproom. He fought the urge to vomit.

He choked the feeling back and picked himself up, wiping his blade on a dead man's tunic. Anyone not dead had fled; all except her. Garrett couldn't bear to look at her. He was staggering toward the door when her voice stopped him.

"You wouldn't leave me now, would you? Not after what you've done for me."

Numb, he turned toward her and found her studying him with an unperturbed air.

Garrett shook his head. "I didn't do it for you, and I'm no one you want to be caught with. The Watch is sure to be on the way here."

"Nonsense," she said, and walked toward him. She ripped a strip of her torn bodice free as she approached and used it to wipe the blood from his brow. "Besides, you'll be caught in no time if you wander around looking like this. Come with me and I'll take you somewhere you can clean yourself up and hide until dawn."

CHAPTER FOUR

He knew it was selfish to go with her. She could be caught up in his troubles should the city watch find him. But he was too exhausted and emotionally drained to refuse her as she led him through the front door and pulled him toward the alley next to the inn.

She hurried him to the far end of the unlit alley and then across the adjoining street, slipping into another pool of shadow. From there, they continued in the same direction down a second darkened alley.

Garrett glanced at the woman and found her watching him as she maneuvered them effortlessly through the gloom. Her luminous eyes seemed even brighter beneath the night sky, and her pale skin now practically glowed, accentuating her exotic features and hollow cheeks. Her gaze made him uncomfortable.

It gave him the feeling, impossible as it was, that she knew his secrets.

"Where are you taking me?" he asked as they turned sharply, the alley opening onto a side street.

She returned her attention to their surroundings. "A quiet place where you can get some rest," she said. Then, after a pause, "Do you mind if I ask you something?"

"What is it?"

She looked deeply into his eyes again, without breaking her stride. "Why do you feel shame?"

Garrett surprised himself by answering, "I suppose I shouldn't. Gods only know what they would have done to you if I hadn't been there. But... I didn't need to kill them all."

She laughed lightly. "I'm sure they all deserved to die." She shook her head once. "But you misunderstand my question. I don't mean shame for what happened back there. What is it that's come before that troubles you so?"

He searched for an explanation and settled on the least damning. "I'm sure you're innocent of the ways of war, but those men were not the first I've killed. I've seen battle. Many battles. But something has changed. Now when I hold steel in my hand... I lose myself. And I can't always remember what I've done."

Touching his chest lightly, she peered around the corner into the next street and raised a finger to her lips. Seconds later, booted footsteps echoed—the city watch. Three guards in rust-colored cloaks walked swiftly past the alley's mouth, unaware of their presence.

Once they were out of earshot, she turned her uncanny citrine eyes on him again. "But why do you dwell on this? Beasts kill. They feel no shame over it. Why should you?"

Her questions frightened him for reasons he couldn't explain. Like icy fingers, they reached for the door to something he wished to keep locked away, even from himself. He searched futilely for an answer. Finally, he responded softly with a question of his own. "Aren't we more than beasts?"

Her eyes lingered on his. He could not read her expression.

Without answering, she took him by the hand and brought him along as she exited the alley to their right. Her hand was surprisingly cool and unyielding.

His eyes darted to both sides of the street, but she walked as if she had no concerns about being seen.

Lost in his own thoughts, he followed her for another block as she guided him.

Her unsettling questions and her casual attitude toward violence filled him with unease.

Desperate to shake off the heavy feeling of malaise swallowing him, he asked, "What is your name?"

She gave him a sidelong smile that didn't touch her luminous eyes. "Lassandra."

CHAPTER FIVE

It was eerily quiet when she brought him to a halt before the iron-bound door of a two-story, dilapidated house in a darkened cul-de-sac. All the windows were shuttered, and no light shone from within. He waited for her to knock, but instead she produced a key and unlocked the door.

"Come inside, but watch your step," she warned. "I have but one candle, and I'm afraid I've left it upstairs."

His nostrils twitched as he stepped over the threshold. The smell of perfume inside was cloying.

Garrett could see nothing of the interior, but Lassandra reached back and took his hand, pulling him gently forward, until his foot bumped into the bottom riser of a staircase.

The incongruence of her having a key suddenly gave him pause. He couldn't risk being seen or questioned by the owners of the house.

"Are you a servant here?" he queried.

Her hand abruptly let go of his.

"Why would you think that?" she replied, her voice husky and unexpectedly close to his ear.

"Well," he stumbled, "because you're a..." he struggled to find a kinder word that would not offend her, but nothing occurred to him, and an awkward stillness followed. He imagined her gaze upon him, somehow penetrating the darkness, her face a mask of silent disapproval.

Just when he felt he couldn't bear her unspoken outrage any longer, her laughter washed over him. He felt her fingers twine with his own again, and she led him up the staircase. He had to grab the railing to keep from stumbling, but she seemed to move steadily and confidently.

She let go of his hand when they reached the landing. A single ray of light shone through an aperture high in the stairwell, though it did nothing to illuminate the staircase. Looking up through the narrow window, he saw the moon, distant and removed, and felt a warm wave of melancholy return.

"You are still troubled?" Lassandra asked.

Yes, he was troubled. Where to begin?

"I'm... not a good man," he haltingly reflected aloud. "I mean, it isn't just the men I've killed. Other soldiers..."

Silence.

Garrett struggled to continue. "War isn't just armies killing each other. Sometimes... sometimes they're ordered to attack villages. Told to spare no one. Not the elders. Not the women. Not the..."

Suppressed memories surged forward in his mind, overlapping with each other until a single image dominated the others—the hut. Garrett grabbed a fistful of his own hair and twisted it until it faded.

Lassandra said nothing. Whether she was patiently waiting for him to continue or struck speechless with revulsion, he had no way of knowing.

His voice cracked as he continued. "Not even the children, but I... I never..." He was thankful for the darkness now as hot tears dripped down his cheeks.

"I see," Lassandra said, taking his hand again. "Why don't you have a seat while I change?"

He let her lead him again until his shin pressed into the soft cushion of a settee. She slowly but firmly turned him, guiding him onto the seat before releasing him.

Garrett wiped his tears quickly, cursing his own weakness and feeling ashamed of allowing her to witness it. It cut him even deeper because he couldn't see how she was judging him for it. Was she afraid? Did she despise him?

He reached out to his left, fumbling for a table or other furniture that might hold the candle she had mentioned earlier. There was nothing but the arm of the settee.

"What do you think of me?" he asked, fearing her answer, but none came from the lightless room. "Am I still no worse than a beast?" Vulnerability consumed him.

In the darkness the silence itself seemed an accusation.

"Do you think I am a monster?" he asked, his voice cracking.

Still there was no reply.

The low sound of wind against shutters revealed the presence of a window several feet to his right. If only he could reach it and let in the moonlight he'd glimpsed from the stairs.

Garrett shuffled toward the sound of the wind and the shutters that must be there, anxious to see Lassandra's face. He tried to brace himself for her judgment, fear, or disgust—whatever her expression might reveal.

As he passed the end of the settee, his leg struck something unexpectedly solid. "Lassandra?" he whispered, heart quickening. The faintest rustle of fabric followed, then a heavy thud on the floor. He hesitated, listening for any sign she might be hurt, but she remained silent.

He went to the window as quickly as he dared, found the latch securing the shutters, flipped it, and pushed them outward. Moonlight streamed in, illuminating half the room.

Garrett looked to the floor where he had heard the thud, expecting to see Lassandra, but to his shock, it was a bearded man in a green silk doublet and hose. The dead man's eyes were open. His pallor was bloodless, but the same could not be said for the hideously torn gash in his throat.

Garrett's eyes swept slowly across the room. Piled unceremoniously atop a four-poster bed to his left, its linens stained with different hues of red, were several corpses in varying states of decomposition. Some were dressed in finery, some like paupers, and a few others wore gambesons and even a hauberk, like the one he had discarded just a few days earlier.

A slurping sound drew his attention. Across the room from Garrett, half in shadow, the woman from the butcher shop sat in a high-backed chair. Her chin and the front of her dress were stained with crimson. The swaddling had loosened around the form in her lap, and now he could see the skull of the long-dead infant she held.

At her feet was the source of the slurping. The boy and girl on all fours, bent over a man in a filthy coat. Both had their mouths fastened to the twitching man's throat.

"You think you are broken because you kill?" Lassandra's voice came from the shadows. She stepped forward into the moonlight. Her eyes glowed unnaturally. Her face was like marble. She was naked except for a thick red cloak which looked just like one he had seen earlier in the evening. "Don't worry. Everyone here is a killer of one sort or another. Or is there something else?"

Garrett's body started to tremble. "What is this? What is happening here?"

"Can we keep this one? He was nice to us." It was the woman from the butcher's shop who spoke.

"No, Ysabel," Lassandra's speech sounded distorted, as if her teeth were too large for her mouth. "Just because he gave you some silver, doesn't mean he isn't a monster."

Ysabel smiled then, exposing wickedly pointed teeth. "Maybe he's like us," she countered.

The man at Ysabel's feet had stopped twitching. The children raised their heads from his throat and wiped their scarlet mouths.

"This one's done," said the boy.

Horror dawned on Garrett's face. He shook his head in denial. "Everything I did—I did under orders. Terrible things happen in war!"

Lassandra slowly walked toward him, her eyes locked on his. He could not look away. Could not move.

"You think that absolves you? Because you were under orders when you slaughtered women and children? You think that makes you better than the rapists at the inn?"

She indicated the corpse in the green doublet with a jerk of her head, "Or this sadist who enjoyed hurting penniless whores?"

As Lassandra continued to advance, Ysabel and the children rose to their feet and began to move toward him as well.

Garrett held up his hands in protest. Fresh tears rolled down his cheeks. "I never... I never hurt women or children. It was the mercenaries who did that. Other soldiers. Not me. Never me! That's why I ran. I couldn't stand it anymore!"

Lassandra was close now. "You think you can outrun your sins? That you can buy forgiveness for what you've done with a piece of silver or an act of chivalry? It was men like you who killed Ysabel's baby. Men like you who left them for dead. And dead they would be if I hadn't found them in time and brought them back with my blood."

"I would never hurt women and children!"

Lassandra reached him then and her cold hand gripped him fiercely by the back of his neck, causing him to cry out. Bent backward, he was helpless, his spine arching painfully in the wrong direction. His eyes were wide with panic as he looked up.

"Only your blood can pay for your sins. But are you a monster or simply a beast?"

Lassandra's mouth opened like a cobra's, exposing serrated fangs.

They sank into his neck—and he remembered.

Huts burned. Bodies were piled in the middle of the village center like cordwood. Garrett stood motionless, staring wide-eyed at the bedlam surrounding him. Dark-eyed mercenaries dragged villagers from their huts and grim-faced soldiers set the thatched roofs ablaze.

Someone grabbed Garrett roughly by the chainmail gorget of his hauberk. His eyes focused. It was the sergeant.

"Oy! Get yer lazy ass in there and kill whoever's inside!"

Garrett staggered backward toward the hut. His sword hand shook as he used it to push open the door.

The small interior was divided by a crude partition of rough logs, inset with a doorless opening. Garrett lurched into the center of the room, his heart thudding, grateful the hut was empty.

He had just begun to turn when a figure burst from the other room and crashed into him, something clutched in its hand.

Too late, Garrett saw the tear-streaked face of a young woman. Her mouth was open, her eyes round with shock. He recoiled, and his sword tore free from her chest.

She dropped to the floor. A crooked stick fell from her hand—her last, futile defense. Gurgling, she took a final rasping breath.

Screams rang out from the partition doorway—children, a boy and a girl.

"No!" Garrett cried. His vision began to turn black at the edges, closing in on him.

"No!" Garrett's voice broke in the present. "Not the children... it was the screaming... I couldn't bear the screaming..."

Lassandra lifted her red mouth from his throat, fixing him with her luminous stare just for a second before tossing him to the floor in front of Ysabel and the children. The three of them fell upon him in a frenzy of thirst.

EPILOGUE

It was several hours past sunset when the covered wagon rounded a low hill, and lights became visible up ahead. The noisy, iron-shod wheels rattled to a stop as the driver brought his pair of mules to a halt.

There were two men in the road. They wore hauberks and carried long spears. One soldier wore an umber surcoat over his armor. He brandished his spear in a two-handed grip toward the driver and the woman seated next to him on the bench. The other soldier, who carried a torch, held his spear casually at his side in his other hand.

The driver turned his head and looked toward the campfire set back a dozen yards from the road. He counted seven more men, seated around the fire. Beyond it was a large tent.

The soldier with the torch came closer, causing one of the mules to snort. He raised the torch high and took a long appraising look at the woman on the wagon, starting with her hips and working his way upward. When his gaze reached her face, he grinned. His focus quickly turned toward the driver then, and he seemed to be looking for any sign of a weapon. Apparently satisfied that there were none, he looked to the woman again. "Where might you be going at such an hour?"

It was the driver who responded, speaking in halting Gauldish, "We are just returning to our village."

"I believe the corporal was addressing the *lady*," the second soldier said tersely.

The woman's voice was cool, but carried the same Beshan accent as the driver. "As my companion said, we are returning to our village."

"You're headed the wrong way then, love." The first soldier sneered. "Ain't no village no more down this road. Only thing comes down this road is outlaws and escapees. It's dangerous in the dark. You should bed down here for the night, then head back the way you came in the morning."

The other men at the campfire were on their feet, headed toward the wagon. Only one of them wore armor. The rest were in loose-fitting shirts and trousers.

One man carried an oil lantern. He whistled when he saw the woman. "Did you tell them about the toll, Ott?"

"I was just offering our protection for the night. I hadn't gotten round to the toll yet."

Several of the men laughed. The one carrying the lantern made his way toward the rear, along with two of the others.

"You don't have to do this," the driver said evenly. "You can do the right thing and just let us pass."

The surcoat-wearing soldier thrust his spear within inches of the driver's face then. "Get the *fok* down from there!" he shouted. "Tell us what we can do will you?"

The woman reached out and let her hand settle on the driver's leg.

"It's all right," he said. He climbed down and stood in the road.

A chuckle sounded from the back of the wagon. "Well, well, well. Ott, we have another fine lass back here! This one's got a couple of brats with her, but that's no matter."

Ott grinned at the driver. "This is a very fortunate night indeed for—" Then his brows sprang up. "I know you!" He turned to the soldier in the surcoat. "It's the *fokken* deserter!"

Garrett shook his head and dropped his feigned accent. "You could have just done the right thing."

The wagon jolted. A man's scream tore through the night as something heavy slammed into the frame. Wood groaned. The whole rig shook.

All the rest of the men, save the two standing before Garrett, raced toward the back of the wagon. There were a couple of dull thuds in quick succession as bodies hit the hard-packed road. Blades rasped free of their scabbards, followed by the sounds of snapping bones and tearing flesh. Men screamed, high and desperate.

Ott turned to look as two men fled toward the campfire. Ysabel loped after them on all fours, quickly catching up to them and taking one to the ground.

Lassandra leaped from the wagon and wrapped her legs around the waist of the surcoat-wearing soldier, her claws tangled in his hair. His knees buckled and he went down on his back with a fountain of crimson spraying from his throat.

Ott's face was ghostly white when he turned back toward Garrett. A metal tinkling sound caused the soldier to look down. Garrett's hand was wrist-deep in the soldier's chest, having punched a hole in his mail as if it were no more substantial than an eggshell. He squeezed Ott's heart, but not too hard. He wanted to look into the bastard's eyes and see the panic as his heart fought to pump life through his body.

"You could have done the right thing many times," Garrett said in a voice that didn't sound like his own. He found it difficult to speak while his fangs bristled from his mouth.

He looked admiringly at Lassandra as she finished drinking from her victim, wiped her mouth, and smiled at him.

He turned back to Ott's horrified face and watched him sputter and choke on his own lifeblood.

Garrett smiled. Despite his best intentions, there were those in the world that just needed killing.

He dropped Ott's corpse like a rotten sack of grain just as the children joined him and Ysabel returned. Lassandra rose to her feet. All of them were splattered in red.

His eyes lingered over each of them—the two pale, ravenous children; Ysabel with her tragic, haunted face; and Lassandra with her unnatural, unshakable calm. His new, bloody family.

While it wasn't anything he could have ever imagined, it was a fresh start nonetheless.

And he was filled with a sense of purpose.

Of righteous fury.

He would die to protect them.

He would kill to protect them.

And the devil take anyone who wished to challenge them.

DESERT FANG

PROLOGUE

In the Days Before the Fall of Al-Zahirah

Naäb al-Sahra's presence coiled with disdain in the Malqarym's mind as the delegates filed into the throne room, in the royal palace of Al-Zahirah.

The Qarym-Shah, sovereign of Za'sharad—the desert kingdom east of Al-Zahirah—walked with his head held high, pleased with himself. The middle-aged Shah was bareheaded, his close-clipped gray hair and beard giving him a regal austerity. He wore a white silk kaftan with a purple sash draped over one shoulder. His three bodyguards, serious men weathered by years in the sun, wore leather harnesses over their kaftans, conical steel caps on their heads, and broad, curved swords at their belts.

A large olivewood banquet table occupied the center of the room, covered with delicacies. Jaharin, the Malqarym of Al-Zahirah, sat at its head, massaging his temple with his left hand to hold the throbbing at bay. He neither stood nor acknowledged his royal guests.

Thirty paces behind Jaharin and the table stood a pair of folding screens, painted with scenes of oases. Between these screens was a large set of double doors, gilt with gold, matching those the Shah and his retinue had just passed through. The chamber's white walls were divided into thirds by two rows of slender, fluted columns. Large arched windows ran the entire length of the wall to the Malqarym's left.

Though the windows stood open on the palace's upper floor, the air remained stiflingly hot, and the perfume worn by his new wife, Sarimeh, seated at his left, was inflaming his senses more than usual.

Seated to his right, his younger brother, Nasiq, chewed a mouthful of dates, the sound grinding Jaharin's teeth. Why did he have to be burdened with such an uncouth lout?

Nasiq leaned in. "I must admit, you were right to hold out for peace. I was rash to think otherwise. This is why you were chosen to be the Malqarym."

A voice only he could hear rasped in the Malqarym's ear. *"Don't listen to that covetous traitor,"* Nab al-Sahra whispered. *"Going to war with Al-Zahirah's enemies is the only thing that pretentious fool has ever been right about."*

Nasiq smiled broadly, unaware of the storm behind his brother's eyes. "I see you wore your wedding gift," he said, indicating the scimitar Jaharin wore at his hip in a bejeweled scabbard. The slender sword was only slightly curved, compared to the heavier blades of the Sha's bodyguards. An oval black opal was inset in the pommel.

The Malqarym gave his younger brother a tight-lipped smile.

"Are you all right, my lord?" Nasiq asked, brow furrowed. "You do not seem yourself today."

"All will soon be well," Jaharin answered.

His wife grasped his hand gently. "Beloved, Nasiq is right. You do not look well. Perhaps we should show our guests to their apartments, and you can reconvene with them in the evening. It will be cooler then, and I am sure they would appreciate the chance to freshen up after their long journey."

Hearing the concern in her voice, Jaharin's eyes softened. He felt confused, and his head ached.

"Don't fall for her lies," Nab al-Sahra said, his voice slithering through Jaharin's mind like a serpent. *"She bathes you in sweet poison, softening you against your brother's schemes."*

Sarimeh smiled sweetly, awaiting his reply.

"We're not leaving this room until I am finished," he said, lips curling back as he squeezed her hand fiercely and cast it off.

Her eyes widened. She leaned back in her chair, taken aback by his harshness.

The Qarym-Shah bowed before taking his seat at the table. "Your highness, you honor us by allowing us to join you in your house." His three bodyguards bowed and backed away from the table, taking a semicircular position, arms crossed, less than a dozen feet from their sovereign.

The Malqarym placed his fingertips together in front of his face, elbows on the table, leaning his nose against his folded hands.

"What are you waiting for?" Nāb al-Sahra needled.

An awkward silence fell over the room, the Qarym-Shah growing visibly uncomfortable under the Malqarym's glare.

Nasiq placed a hand on his shoulder. "Brother?" his voice was full of concern.

Jaharin turned, staring at the offending hand as if it were a viper. "You forget yourself... *little* brother. I am still your Malqarym."

Stung, Nasiq removed his hand from his shoulder. "I meant no offense, Malqarym."

"We have brought you many fine gifts to celebrate your wedding," the Shah said, attempting to break the tension. "Thirty of our finest camels. Ten crates of silk. A hundred gold ingots. I only regret we were not able to attend the celebration in person."

Nāb al-Sahra scoffed. *"This dog thinks to buy your favor, as if you were nothing more than a common whore. Do not suffer him to live."*

The Malqarym nodded to his palace guards. They moved swiftly to the double doors, shutting them before dropping a heavy iron bar into place.

"Yes," Nāb al-Sahra urged.

"What is the meaning of this?" the Shah demanded. His bodyguards reached for their sword hilts.

"Brother?" Nasiq queried again, his expression a mixture of concern and bewilderment.

Jaharin struck him across the face. "I told you to address me as Malqarym!"

Nasiq accepted the blow, dumbfounded, but Jaharin's wife began to cry, startled by his bizarre behavior.

The Malqarym made a slashing motion across his throat. A trio of archers stepped from behind the folding screens, loosing arrows into the torsos of the Shah's bodyguards. Before they could recover, a second volley struck.

Chaos broke loose as the chamber exploded into violence.

Nasiq staggered out of his chair, knocking it over to clatter on the tiles. The Shah ran toward one of the windows but was grabbed by two palace guards.

The Malqarym stalked toward the captive, fingers stroking the hilt of his scimitar.

"Yes!" Nab al-Sahra cried in exultation. *"At last!"*

"Hold him down," the Malqarym ordered.

Guards forced the Shah onto his knees, head down, arms outstretched at his sides.

"Brother!" Nasiq cried, forgetting himself yet again as he stepped between Jaharin and the Shah. "This is not the way."

"Make up your mind, little brother!" the Malqarym spat, foam flecking his lips. "You wanted war with our neighbors, remember? Well, this is just the start! First, Za'sharad. Next, Mar-Üd, and the rest."

"Not like this. I thought a show of strength was right when you first ascended Father's throne. But this is barbarism. You were right to seek peace through negotiation."

"He is a traitor," Nab al-Sahra hissed.

The Malqarym drew his curved sword. The opal in the pommel seemed to swirl, as if it were filled with liquid—and something else.

"I cannot let you do this!" Nasiq pleaded.

"Seize him!" the Malqarym shouted. Two guards restrained Nasiq.

Jaharin turned to the downed Shah, who was praying in his native tongue. His bloodshot eyes fixed on the Shah as he raised the scimitar overhead. Sunlight gleamed on it through the open window. The sword flashed downward, and a scarlet arc sprayed across the front of the Malqarym's robe. The Shah's head hit the tiled floor with a sickening thud and rolled to a stop.

"Oh, what have you done, you fool?" Nasiq cried, his face pallid. "Once word of this treachery gets out, all the nations will unite and come against us as one."

The Malqarym turned toward Nasiq. "Let them come. As for you, you won't have to worry about it anymore. Put him down."

The guards holding Nasiq looked alarmed. "Sire?"

Sobbing, Sarimeh rushed toward Jaharin, clutching his arm. "No! No! You cannot do this! He is your bro—"

Blood trickled from her mouth. Her eyes glazed over as she looked down to see the scimitar buried deep in her side, the jeweled hilt protruding from her ribs. She crumpled to the floor.

The guards' grip on Nasiq loosened in surprise, and he shook them off, his eyes wild. In one swift, desperate motion, he seized the sword from one guard's scabbard and swung it hard across Jaharin's neck.

The Malqarym's body collapsed, his severed head landing grotesquely beside it.

Tears streamed down Nasiq's face as the stunned guards recoiled in horror. He dropped the sword with a clatter and sank to one knee beside Sarimeh's still form where she lay in a gathering pool of crimson.

Quiet now, the chamber seemed to hold its breath.

"Why?" he asked no one, distraught. "What madness possessed him?"

Nasiq reached out, trembling, and grasped the hilt of Jaharin's scimitar, still lodged in her side.

As he pulled the blade free, a sharp pain seared through the center of his palm. He turned his hand over and saw a narrow gash there.

He hesitated for a moment, then reached for the hilt once more. A tremor ran up his arm. He felt the weight of something ancient, hateful, and hungry.

Nāb al-Sahra's laughter echoed in the silence—unheard by any but Nasiq. It throbbed once in his hand. Then the whispering began.

CHAPTER ONE

Dara's lithe, dark-clad form clung to the temple wall, high above the alley. Her strong fingers gripped the masonry, the balls of her feet balancing on the bas-relief of the virgin goddess.

The evening breeze whipped her long, tawny hair across her face. She puffed a stray lock from between her lips, wishing she'd tied it back before tonight's burglary. But her unruly tresses were the least of her concerns.

Kephius, high priest of Sibilee—cult of chastity, purity, and propriety—was supposed to be meditating until midnight. Instead, he'd come staggering in, two hours early, held upright by a painted harlot under each arm and flanked by his eunuch bodyguards. Dara hadn't yet found the strongbox, and now her timing had gone to rot.

Dara had barely managed to dive through the fourth-story window unseen, her cloak snagged on the sill, left fluttering like a banner for any fool to find.

She huffed and lifted one of her feet from Sibilee's head, probing for her next foothold.

A commotion rose in the alley below. Dara stilled herself and cocked an ear downward. Voices were clearly raised in anger, but their words echoed, muffled and lost in the narrow space.

Dara bit her lower lip, trying to steady herself. She didn't want anyone in the alley seeing her, but it was only a matter of moments before the priest, or his bodyguards, noticed his possessions had been rummaged. If anyone were to poke their head out of the window above her and look down, she would be discovered.

She began her descent again, slowly feeling her way down.

A moment later, low enough to drop safely to the ground, she landed silently in a crouch. Now she could make out some of the heated exchange.

"I know what you say about me behind my back!" shouted a man with a nasally whine.

"Have you gone daft, Brenwin?" rumbled another man with a deep voice. "I told you already, we didn't say anything about you."

"Then why did you try to avoid me by hiding in this alley?" the nasally man retorted.

"By the gods, Brenwin, we didn't even know it was you. We just saw someone following us and thought you were a robber," protested a third man. "When did you take to wearing a sword?"

A shrill cry from above cut through the night, halting the voices in the alley. "Someone has been in my chambers!" Then, from the window directly overhead, a clearer shout: "The thieves left something behind—look here!"

Dara cursed under her breath. She wanted nothing to do with the dispute in the alley, but she couldn't risk slipping out near the front of the temple, not with the high priest bellowing from the window. Keeping low in the shadows along the walls of the neighboring temples, she crept toward the argument, careful to avoid the moonlight.

Now she could see the owners of the three voices. A short, pudgy man with a receding hairline and weak chin stood with his hands on his hips, one drifting toward the hilt of a fine-looking scimitar. He was confronting two larger men—one wearing a blue velvet beret, the other adorned with a substantial gold necklace resting on the breast of his silk tunic.

The shorter man cocked his head to one side, as if listening to someone just out of sight. "I know they did!" he hissed.

That was when Dara recognized him. He was a jeweler who owned his own shop. He would never buy jewels from her, but she didn't hold that against him. He was a respectable businessman. Though she didn't know him well, he had always seemed mild and good-natured—nothing like the wild-eyed figure now pacing the alley. His jaw twitched like he was biting back words not meant for anyone else. He kept glancing at empty corners, flinching at things no one else seemed to hear. As he barked his next accusation, he tilted his head again, more sharply this time, like he was straining to catch some low whisper. Something only he could hear.

"Who is he talking to?" the man in the beret asked his companion.

"Gods if I know," answered the necklace wearer. "I think he's gone mad."

Brenwin turned his attention back to them then, spittle flying from his lips as he shouted, "I know you've been stealing my customers! Telling them I've swindled them with inferior stones!" He stepped closer to them. A scrape of metal and then the scimitar was in his hand, pointed at the two larger men.

"Brenwin," the man in the gold necklace said emphatically, "go on home now! I don't know if you've been drinking, but you aren't yourself. That's for sure. Put that sword away before you hurt someone."

"That's just what I intend to do!" the jeweler snapped, then charged, swinging the curved sword.

The man in the beret dodged the clumsy swing and the other man grabbed the jeweler's arm. Together, they forced him back toward the wall of the temple. Brenwin's head slammed against the stone, and the scimitar clattered to the alley. He crumpled and his head smacked against the cobblestones.

"I don't need this kind of trouble," the man in the beret said, his tone distressed.

"Agreed," said the other man. "This never happened."

Together, they ran the other way out of the alley.

Dara rushed to the fallen jeweler. His glassy eyes stared skyward, lifeless. He hardly looked like a back-alley brawler, with his soft hands, rotund waist, and no sign he knew his way around a sword.

The sword in question was well crafted. Tiny sapphires were set in the rounded guard and a large black opal set at the end of the pommel. The scabbard itself was decorated with several little gems.

While Dara had some familiarity with blades, she had little use for swords herself. But this one looked valuable enough to fetch considerable coin; maybe enough to salvage tonight's botched robbery. She took no pleasure in the jeweler's misfortune, but what was done was done. It was the second job gone wrong in recent memory, if she counted the incident with the Giltwarden, which hadn't really been her fault.

Still, the risk of failure was starting to outweigh the rewards, especially after the danger she'd exposed Tamir to. He'd never liked her occupation, even before that.

She removed the man's belt with deft fingers. Snatching the sword up by the hilt, she felt a sharp pain in her palm. To her surprise, she found a cut there, but very little blood. Examining the hilt, she didn't see any sharp edges that would have caused the injury.

Dara shrugged, buckled the belt around her waist, then slipped deeper into the alley toward the back of the temple.

Just as she came even with the rear of the adjacent temples, Dara froze. She could have sworn she heard someone softly whisper her name. She stood perfectly still, ears straining for the whisper that never came again, leaving only chilling silence.

Scoffing at her own skittishness, the young thief got on the move once more. She couldn't afford to be found lurking near the scene of both an attempted robbery and a murder.

Dara slipped into the service lanes and crooked footpaths threaded between the massive temples and the bathhouses crouched behind them. Meant for deliveries and servants, they twisted like arteries through the district—but she knew their ways.

She didn't notice the brief rippling in the surface of the opal in the sword's pommel.

CHAPTER TWO

She took a sharp left behind a spice-merchant's courtyard, fragrant leaves and blossoms wafting from within, and jogged through a shadowed colonnade. A crumbling staircase waited beside a half-collapsed wall, and Dara climbed it soundlessly, the scimitar bumping gently against her hip with every step.

The stair let out on a narrow side street just shy of the front of the temple of the god of fortune.

From there, it was easy to merge with the few faithful still making their way along the Boulevard of Eternity, where the major temples of Saintsward faced one another across the wide avenue. Of all Thiardun's many districts, she despised Saintsward the most. Even the brutal pragmatism of crime-ridden Cheapside made more sense to her than the blind, grating faith that flourished here.

Dara walked with measured steps, doing her best to look like she belonged. She wished the crowd were thicker. A quiet street could be more treacherous than a packed one.

Reaching to pull up her hood, she winced. It was gone, torn off on the high priest's window. A mistake, she chided herself. One that left traces.

Her mouth was dry, and she felt oddly unsettled. She needed a drink, but she knew she should sell the sword as soon as possible.

She would do both and then go to see Tamir. The old sage disapproved of her profession, but after all these years, she still found his fatherly manner comforting.

Somewhat distracted by her contemplation, Dara looked up to see a large, bearded man heading directly toward her. She started to adjust her course, involuntarily, but then it occurred to her... Why should she have to move out of the way?

A bitter edge she didn't fully welcome cut through her thoughts.

Obviously, he could see her just as well as she could see him, but he was a man, so of course he expected her to show deference and demurely step aside.

Look at his fine clothing, new shoes, full purse at his belt. He never wants for anything. Probably on his way to tithe to that fool of a priest.

Head down, unyielding, she plowed straight ahead and collided with the man's broad frame. He was larger than her, and the impact spun her halfway around. She turned the rest of the way to find him facing her, eyes narrowed.

"Watch it!" the man barked.

Dara's face twitched. "Something you want to say to me?"

"Careful how you speak, girl." He straightened his shoulders.

"Am I meant to be frightened?" she asked with a hard grin.

"Show him he's nothing but a worm to be trampled," a voice whispered behind her.

Dara's head snapped around. No one stood there. Only a boxy, horse-driven carriage rattling along the cobbles toward them.

She felt a prickling at the base of her neck. The voice had seemed to stroke the inside of her skull.

"Mind," the man said, with an air of superiority, and she turned to him once more. "You'd do well to know I'm the bailiff of Saintsward."

Her eyes widened as her anger fled. What had she gotten herself into?

"And who might you be, then?" He took a step toward her, grasping for her shoulder, but she stepped back, out of reach.

"Strike him down quickly, before he sends you to the Iron Roost," someone breathed in her ear. The bailiff seemed not to hear it.

Lips parted in surprise, brow furrowed, she glanced to her left and right. "Who said that?"

"Are you touched then?" the bailiff asked, raising an eyebrow. "I did. What is your name?"

"No, I don't mean..." Dara exhaled, glancing at the swiftly approaching carriage. "I'm just a simple believer out for some exercise and contemplation."

The bailiff came toward her more aggressively, but she twisted away. As the carriage swept past, Dara sprang lightly, grasping a handhold near its roof as one foot landed squarely on the narrow rear step.

Shaking his fist, the red-faced bailiff dwindled from her view.

Turbulence stirred within the opal in the sword's pommel again as Na'b al-Sahra seethed and plotted.

CHAPTER THREE

Dara's heartbeat slowed to a normal pace as she listened to the creak of the swaying carriage and rhythmic drumming of the horses' hooves. The smells of the leather curtains over the cabin's windows and sweat from the horses' flanks grounded her, causing her to doubt whether she had really heard the disembodied voice that had spoken to her in the street.

Dara wondered if the stress from her recent failures could make her hear voices. Or if it was a lingering effect of the short time she spent trapped in the Idir—the dream realm of the ghouls.

She was lost in thought when the carriage driver looked back finally. His expression quickly soured.

"Get off, you damn vermin!" he shouted.

Dara's face flushed. She knew she was trespassing, but what right did he have to speak to her so?

She reached for the scimitar belted at her waist. Her fingers brushed the hilt—and recoiled. Her breath caught.

It felt wrong. Not cold or sharp, but sinuous. For a moment, it was as if the sword had reached back.

She looked down and realized what she'd been about to do.

What was she thinking?

Dara dropped from the carriage and watched it race away.

She shook her head. She needed that drink more than ever, but she wasn't far from Yaromir and Bernardo's storefront. Besides, her favorite watering hole, the Quiet Cup, was across the city in The Lanternway, near Tamir's shop.

***

Chewing over the evening's events, she realized she was standing before the Wren.

She lingered outside for a moment and took a deep breath. A sense of dread tightened around her chest at the thought of parting with the sword; but at the same time, she hadn't felt right since finding it, and was eager to be rid of it.

Yaromir and Bernardo had fenced many items for her in the past, without question. They were always discreet, if a little peculiar.

Dara opened the door, and the sound of tinkling chimes greeted her. The shop was warmly illuminated by the pleasant glow from a wooden chandelier laden with many fat candles, hanging from the vaulted ceiling. A pair of oil lamps covered with colored glass also sat on the cherrywood counter at the business end of the interior.

Behind the counter, two matching archways were covered with glass bead curtains.

A mingled bouquet of polished teak, oiled leather, old parchment, and countless other scents greeted her as she walked through the shop, crowded with all sorts of incongruous treasures.

She passed an exquisitely crafted writing desk and thought of Tamir. A preserved, stuffed lizard sat atop a crate, itself stacked upon several others. All manner of garments, including a chain shirt, were draped over various crude mannequins. A glass case displayed assorted bangles and baubles on a swath of velvet, and leaning against one end of the case was the portrait of one of the previous queens of Gauldün. She had seen it here several times before but never thought to ask her name.

She reached the counter just as the shop owners emerged from behind the glass curtains.

On her left was Yaromir, short, fleshy, and bald. He smiled broadly with recognition.

On her right, Bernardo, a tall, wiry figure with a mustache that matched his frame. She had never seen Bernardo smile.

Yaromir spoke first, in good spirits. "My dear girl, what have you got for us this evening? Some jewelry, perhaps?"

Bernardo sniffed.

"Not this time," Dara replied, "but I think you'll be interested." She unbuckled the sword belt.

As she set the weapon upon the counter, a presence crawled forward in her consciousness and murmured, *"That is unwise."*

She looked frantically at each of the shop owners, searching their faces for any sign they'd heard it, but if they had, it did not show.

"Is everything all right, child?" Yaromir asked, concern replacing his earlier mirth.

Bernardo placed a hand under one elbow and stroked his jaw with well-manicured fingers, watching her carefully.

"I just need a drink," Dara answered. "It's been a long night already." She indicated the scimitar with a jerk of her head. "I can tell by the craftsmanship, let alone the jewel in the pommel, that it's got to be worth at least half its weight in silver."

Both shop owners looked down at the sword. Yaromir's hand moved toward the opal.

Dara's nose wrinkled. She swore something had just moved in the stone.

Bernardo's fingers clamped down on Yaromir's wrist just before he could touch the sword. His eyes fixed on the stone in the pommel, which seemed to flicker faintly in the candlelight. "Not this one," he said quietly, voice taut.

Dara caught the sharp edge in his tone but didn't understand the meaning behind it. Whatever it was, Bernardo wasn't about to touch the blade or argue with her over it.

Yaromir looked at his partner, wide-eyed. Bernardo let go of his wrist.

Dara's voice dropped, low and dangerous. "You've bought blades from me before."

"Not like this one," Bernardo replied, his face inscrutable.

"They think they are your betters," Naּb al-Sahra whispered, its hot breath touching the side of her neck. Her face flushed, not unpleasantly.

Her head cocked to the side—not startled this time, but listening. They *did* think they were better than her.

Yaromir looked back and forth between his partner and Dara, a bewildered look on his face.

"What about you, toad?" she said to the shorter man through clenched teeth. "Does he speak for you?"

It was Bernardo who responded first, unmoved by her outburst. "We are not interested in the sword. We cannot help you—even if we wished to. Leave. And may the gods shield you."

Yaromir looked at her sympathetically. "I'm sorry. You're not yourself. Go home. Get some rest."

Something brushed against her mind, like a fellow conspirator. *"Show them,"* the sword goaded her.

Dara stared at the sword for a long moment, holding her breath, unfamiliar urges straining to break free.

Finally, she exhaled, snatched the scimitar from the counter, and practically ran from the shop. She didn't know what was happening to her. Whatever it was, she needed that drink to drown it. *Now.*

CHAPTER FOUR

Dara stood beneath the weathered sign of the Strutting Stag, perched on Cheapside's western edge. The entrance faced the street, but the bulk of the tavern overlooked the dark riverbank below.

She couldn't say how, but she'd ended up here rather than in The Lanternway, where she'd originally intended to go. And she'd chosen this pisshole—the haunt of the Hobblers, a place she normally avoided.

An insane thought occurred to her. Maybe it hadn't been her choice at all—maybe it had been the sword's. The line between the two of them had begun to blur.

She scoffed at herself and opened the door. The damp chill from the river followed her inside.

She strolled through the loud, hazy tavern. It reeked of sweat and smoke. Several heads turned to follow her as she walked toward the bar. Dara recognized a few of them. It seemed they recognized her too. *Good.*

"Wine. Not that watered-down swill you try and pass off either," she growled at the barkeep.

The barkeep's scowl brought color to Dara's cheeks. She felt a gut-twist, like she was riding a wild horse, barreling downhill with no reins.

The barkeep took a small keg from beneath the oak bar and filled a tankard before slamming it down. That steeled her nerves again. She wouldn't be cowed by a lout who owned a gutter joint like this one.

She drained it in one go and it was her turn to slam it onto the bar. "Another."

She turned and surveyed the room. At a table near the far wall, a large oaf with a shaved head sat nursing his own tankard. He had several fading bruises on his face.

She knew this insect—*Kornin*. Dara grinned when she saw the recognition in the thug's glare.

With a last haughty glance, she turned her back to him and picked up her newly filled tankard.

She barely had time for a swallow of it before a thick finger poked her in the back. Dara turned to find Kornin looming over her.

"Can I help you?" her voice dripped venom. Her look was smug. Provoking.

He pointed a finger inches from her nose. "I know your face."

"Very impressive. I wouldn't expect an ant brain like yours to retain anything beyond which end you stuff the food into, and which end it comes out of." She smiled, but her eyes were hard.

Kornin's face purpled. He cracked his knuckles loudly. "I don't like you, bitch."

Her eyes narrowed and the façade of a smile fled. "You won't see me weep. I came to drink, and I'll leave when I'm gods-damned through."

She turned back to the bar and reached for her tankard. A meaty hand grasped her shoulder and spun her back around.

Spittle flew from Kornin's lips. "I said I don't like you! I didn't say you could leave!"

He swung a fist at her, and she ducked—his knuckles struck a cluster of tankards hanging from hooks behind the bar. They clattered to the floor in a clanging cascade. Dara saw Kornin reach for his dagger, but she drove her knee into his groin before he could draw it. He doubled over with a grunt.

She leaned hard against the bar and kicked up into his shoulders with both feet. The force sent him stumbling backward, giving her room.

Somehow, her sword was in her hand. She blinked at it, surprised. Kornin was scum, but she hadn't come here to kill him. Or had she?

While she was distracted, her opponent recovered. He roared with fury, startling her, and came at her with bare steel.

Their swords met with a clash. Steel rang as they exchanged blows.

The oaf was no great swordsman, Dara could tell, but neither was she, and he had the advantage of size and strength.

She was driven backward, savagely, and soon found herself with her back against the bar, their swords locked before them. Kornin grinned as he leaned his weight onto the weapons. It was a common tactic of his, using his great bulk to pin an opponent and squeeze the air out of them—she'd seen him do it before.

Dara had a two-handed grip on the scimitar, but the tendons in her arm were on fire as she strained to keep his heavier blade at bay.

Teeth grinding together, she released one hand from the hilt and reached for the dagger under her sleeve. But as she did, the opal in the pommel of her sword caught her eye.

The opal swirled like a tempest, and at its heart, a spectral eye opened. Something cold and unseen seized her wrist—pulling it toward her dagger. *"Stab him,"* a voice whispered. *"But leave the final blow for me."*

"By the black gods!" Kornin shouted. She saw the look on his face, followed his eyes, and saw that he too had seen something in the pommel stone.

Sanity flashed in Dara's eyes. Instead of her dagger, she reached for the tankard of wine on the bar top and flung it into Kornin's face.

The oaf shouted, blinking the stinging wine out of his eyes. Dara felt the pressure against her sword slacken, and she pivoted out of the way. Kornin lurched forward, and she slammed the tankard into his temple. His head collided with the bar, and he landed in an unmoving heap.

Dara gasped for air. Her face no longer flushed with rage, but with the sharp burn of exertion. She stood over her unconscious enemy, looking down at him. She could end him now. And disturbingly, part of her wanted to.

"Yes," Nab al-Sahra purred, its voice caressing the nape of her neck. *"Do it."*

She took a deep breath and shivered. What was she doing? She wasn't a killer. This was not her.

Her gaze flicked around the room. All the other patrons were standing, staring at her.

She rushed past them, out the door and down the steps. Acting on instinct, she ran toward the back of the tavern.

Hefting the sword, she readied to hurl it into the river.

"You are mine," a seething voice echoed in her head. Icy fingers closed over her own, squeezing tight around the sword's hilt.

Her teeth clenched as she struggled to open her hand and drop the weapon over the rushing water. The icy grip held fast, but now she felt two others tighten around her throat, cutting off her breath.

Sweat ran down her face. Try as she might, she could not let go.

"Do not resist," Nāb al-Sahra said soothingly, in stark contrast to the punishment inflicted.

Her vision began to dim. Desperate, she found the scabbard at her belt and plunged the sword inside.

Instantly, the icy hands released her.

She turned from the river, breathing hard. Tamir—he'd know what to do if anyone could. He had to. Before this thing took her for good.

CHAPTER FIVE

Tamir, scribe, sage, and occasional practitioner of magic, hailed from the Blistering Lands—a desert realm on the southern continent, across the Mist Sea from Gauldün.

His olive-toned face was lined with worry.

They stood in the warm glow from a wooden, candlelit chandelier hung above Tamir's cluttered workspace: a loft crowded with a large worktable, shelves, and other furniture. It overlooked the shop below, packed with his precious tomes and scrolls. Dara's comfortable chair sat empty, its back to the railing, opposite his own.

"Set it on the worktable," he said cautiously.

"I'll try," she said warily. "Don't touch it whatever you do."

The girl he thought of as a daughter stood near the table, swaying indecisively.

Tamir pushed aside a manuscript and the open tome he had been copying it into.

Eyes closed and jaw clenched, Dara laid it on the table, releasing the blade but not the hilt.

"It won't let me go," she said finally. Her complexion was pale, and her brow was damp with perspiration.

"It?" he asked, a cold sensation touching his spine.

"It's alive. It—I can't explain it. It's whispering to me right now. It's telling me to hurt you."

The old shopkeeper's eyes narrowed, and he took a small step backward.

"Don't worry. I won't."

Tamir stroked his beard, brow furrowed. "Where did I put... ah." He walked to a bookcase and removed a tome with copper plates attached to the front and back covers. Laying it on the table, he found the page he was looking for. He took up a piece of chalk and drew a circle around the sword, pausing at three points to inscribe runes that joined the curved lines.

"What is that meant to do? Keep the evil in? I think it's too late for that already."

"No, no," he replied, working a pulley to lower the wooden chandelier over the table. "If I cannot, as you say, touch it, which I am sure is wise advice, then I will need a conduit to reach the sword another way." He snuffed out each candle in the chandelier, save for one, which he removed and placed on the opposite side of the table, atop one of the runes. Then he placed each of his hands on one of the two remaining glyphs.

"Please be careful," Dara warned. Even in the shadows, he could see the worry in her eyes.

"Do not fear," he said, doing his best to comfort her.

Tamir focused on the only light in the now dim room—the single candle across from him. He began to pray softly in the old tongue.

Everything else fell into darkness. Everything but the flickering flame.

Then the flame, too, dulled and stretched into a vision of another time and place.

***

A withered old mystic in black silk robes and a cloth headwrap marked with sigils sat alone in a cramped, dim chamber, surrounded by peculiarities.

There was a knock at the chamber door. "Wise one, it is I Nasiq," the visitor announced in a regal tone.

The old man lifted his head from the parchment he had been entertaining himself with, a sly expression on his face. Rolling up the scroll and setting it on a shelf, he answered, "Ah, enter, my prince. You are most welcome."

The door opened and in stepped a young man with rich brown skin. "I am glad to find you in your chambers."

"Oh, Nasiq?" The mystic peered at the young prince. "What is it that troubles the heir apparent to the throne of Al-Zahirah?"

"Heir presumptive," Nasiq corrected. "My brother is to be married tomorrow, after all. There is no reason to think he won't be blessed with a son."

"Ah, you are correct, my prince." The mystic bowed his head. "All the same, it seems that you came here with a need."

The prince paced before the old man's desk. "In truth, it is my brother. I understand he wants peace, maybe even more than our father did. If he doesn't begin his reign with strength, I fear it'll haunt us for years to come. Perhaps you could talk to him. Cast the bones for him. Tell him that I am right about this."

"If only it were that easy," the old man replied. "My powers of divination are well known, but I cannot tell the new Malqarym how he must rule. However, I have counseled him on this. I too think he should bring Al-Zahirah's neighbors to heel and then rule with mercy once strength is assured. Alas, he has too much of his father in him... many blessings upon his name."

"Is there nothing you can do then?" Nasiq flung his hands in frustration. "Perhaps a charm or a potion that will help him see things more clearly?"

"I am afraid not, my prince. Even without the threat of death, I lack the means for such magic."

"I see," said Nasiq. He looked over the scores of curiosities lining the mystic's shelves. "Perhaps there is still something you can help me with."

"Name it, my prince. If it is within my power, consider it done."

"I need a gift for my brother. I didn't give him anything when he ascended to Malqarym, and now he is to be wed. I want to give him something to put all this behind us and show him that there is no bad blood between us."

The mystic rested his chin on his fist, staring at nothing in concentration. "Ah!" he said suddenly. "I know just the thing."

He motioned for the prince to follow, and they walked to a display case on the other side of the room. Within the case, a magnificent scimitar was displayed next to a bejeweled scabbard. Tiny sapphires were set in the sword's rounded guard, and a large black opal was inset in the hilt.

The prince grabbed the sides of the glass lid immediately and began to raise it.

"You mustn't!" the mystic warned, grabbing the prince's wrists, causing the younger man to glare at the offending hands. To touch a member of the royal family without permission was a capital offense.

"I meant no disrespect, my prince." The old man bowed his head. With a hidden smirk, he added, "It is only that it is an ill omen to hold a sword intended for a Malqarym, with the exception of the craftsman who forged it, of course."

The prince nodded and removed his hands from the glass case.

"I will have it sent to His Majesty in a gilded sandalwood box, so that no one may be tempted to spoil the gift," the old man said.

The prince began to reply, but the vision faded and Tamir found himself in complete and impenetrable darkness. A hot wind blew across his face.

"You would seek to learn about me?" asked an oily voice from the dark.

"That depends," Tamir said cautiously. "Are you the sword?"

Menacing laughter peeled all around the scribe. "I am not a sword, but the weapon is me... for now. Others have called me Na'b al-Sahra. You may do so as well."

"What do you want with Dara?" Tamir felt an unnatural cold, shaped like fingers, touching his brow. He swept his hand across his face but nothing was there.

"Her obedience," the voice replied. "I want her to plunge me into someone's heart. Slash me across another's throat. She's trying to resist me, but you should warn her against such futility. Else yours may be the first head she takes."

"I will not let you have her," the scribe retorted, defiant. "Not now or ever!"

The wicked laughter came again, but quieter. It sounded like it was right beside Tamir's head, and he felt something frigid, coiling around his upper body.

"When she grasped my hilt and felt my bite, a pact was sealed. She cannot be released until she takes a life. Whatever happens after that is dependent on the strength of her will. But know this, Al-Zahirah wasn't the first or last kingdom to fall at my influence. What chance does a mere girl have to resist me?"

"Why are you doing this? Why Dara? She is not a ruler. She does not have a kingdom!" Tamir shouted.

"Why?" the unctuous voice said, this time from within his own mind. *"Because I have been trapped within this blade for millennia, and the bloodshed of your pathetic mortal race is a sweet distraction."*

A giant, luminous eye suddenly opened before Tamir. Around it, shadows writhed, forming faint shapes—claws and twisting tendrils of smoke, too quick and indistinct to fully comprehend, but enough to make his blood run cold.

Something alien reached into his mind and snapped his consciousness into connection with Nab al-Sahra's.

Tamir caught glimpses of the demon's handiwork across the ages—the ruin of noble warriors, the corruption of just kings, the fall of empires. He saw the wickedness of the thing, understood what it desired, and felt its bloodlust. The chaotic visions and impulses flooding his mind were overwhelming.

Screaming, he opened his eyes and found himself staring into the candle flame once more.

"Tamir! Are you all right?" Dara cried, snatching the sword from the table and sheathing it.

The scribe walked to his chair and sank into it, his head in his hands.

"My child, this blade is imbued with an evil spirit. A demon. The legends of Mar-Üd refer to such a thing as an Ifrit. It seeks to dominate you. To twist you into a murderer."

Dara paced in front of her chair. "Tell me how to rid myself of the damned thing."

"Your only hope is to appease its bloodlust. Only in that instant, when it is drunk on someone's death, do you have even the faintest hope of walking away."

Her lips parted. "What are you suggesting I do, Tamir?"

He looked at her with haunted eyes. "I saw them—all of them. The ones who bore it before you. None escaped until the blade had fed. Only then, when the demon was sated, was there a fleeting chance to cast it away. Few had the will to even try; fewer still succeeded."

Dara shook her head slowly, a troubled expression clouding her face. "I may be a thief, but I am not a killer."

Tamir stood and gently placed his hands on her arms. "It is the only way. If you do not give it what it wants voluntarily, it will drive you mad and take the choice away from you. It is not a question of *if* you will take a life... but rather, *whose* life you will take."

"Or I could be killed instead. I quarreled with someone at the Stag earlier this evening. He almost got the best of me. Even if I were willing to kill someone just for a chance to be free of the accursed blade, there's no guarantee I'll be the victor."

It was Tamir's turn to pace. "I do not like it either."

"And even if I did survive, who am I to decide whose life is worth less than my own? If I knew for sure the man was a ruthless killer, maybe I could live with that. But even if I could be certain, those kinds of men usually travel with others like themselves."

She took a decanter from a nearby bookcase and sank into her chair.

Seeing her intention, Tamir grabbed two wooden cups from another shelf and took the other chair.

Dara leaned forward, a thoughtful look on her face as she poured the wine. Without a word, she downed the contents of her cup.

"Of course," she said, finally, breaking the silence. "It's the only way."

"What do you mean, my dear?"

Dara refilled her cup, leaned back, and told Tamir her plan.

CHAPTER SIX

Dara woke just after midday, sweating and clutching the demonic scimitar.

Tamir looked as bad as she felt, his eyes dark and sunken, his face slack with exhaustion. She knew he must have been up the entire night trying to find any alternative to her plan, whether mystical or mundane. She'd found him slumped over his worktable, sleeping on a pile of books.

They had left Tamir's cluttered shop with few words between them, said even less while tramping through The Lanternway, and now walked side by side into an alley at the northern edge of Cheapside's largest bazaar.

Forgotten by the duke's laws and mostly ignored by the city watch of Thiardun, the bazaar and the tangle of alleyways spilling from it were a honeycomb of vice—brothels, gambling dens, and even darker delights tucked behind every painted door and drawn shutter.

Men who had run out of silver at the tables—or simply run out of luck—were tossed unceremoniously into the gutter. Hollow-eyed merchants beckoned any passerby with a coin into their darkened shops, where the air reeked of sour bodies and smoke, to sample a bit of dreamblossom.

The pair finally reached their destination, a flight of stone steps that led to a vault beneath the bazaar. As they descended, their ears were assaulted by shouts of exultation and hoarse cries from the defeated and wounded, strained with pain and exhaustion.

Though the massive space below lay hidden from the sun, there was no breeze to cool the narrow walkways between the fighting pits. The heat accumulated throughout the day, in addition to that generated by so many bodies in such a cramped space, had nowhere to go.

Dara's gut tightened as she glanced around, suddenly questioning the wisdom of her plan. In the light of day, it seemed far less reasonable.

She tugged at Tamir's robe, and they pressed their way through the throng of wild-eyed spectators. Dara's own eyes watered at the pungent stink of unwashed bodies.

Vacant spaces broke up the chaos of the crowd, seemingly at random, each about twenty feet across, where wagerers gathered around pits sunk into the vault floor. A small, circular aperture above each pit let in a single shaft of sunlight, illuminating the combatants while those cheering or cursing above jostled each other in shadow.

Dara looked down to her left as they passed the first pit, where two grizzled, weary combatants struggled against one another, their faces devoid of hope or spirit.

They passed another pit on their right. A slender youth lay on its sandy bottom, an oozing wound in his side. An older veteran stood over him, covering him with a spear. The watchers above cried out for blood, but the veteran shook his head in disgust and tossed his weapon aside.

Dara could not kill these men—not even if she bested them in a fight. She didn't know them, nor could she judge whether they deserved to die.

Midway through the vault, a low wall enclosed a crack in the stone at their feet. It was at least three yards wide, and as Dara leaned over the edge, she saw only darkness. The faint sound of rushing water, far below, was barely discernible over the cacophony of the throng surrounding her. She vaguely remembered something about a collapse, years ago. A sinkhole had opened, dropping away into an underground river, hundreds of feet beneath the city. She wondered how long it would be before the rest of the bazaar followed.

Dara was jolted suddenly as a cluster of men escorted an armored warrior across the vault toward a pit on the far side. Her teeth ground together as outrage built up within her. She took a deep breath and reminded herself it was the sword's influence—not her own true emotion she was feeling.

She glanced around for Tamir and saw him a dozen feet away, talking to a flabby, bare-chested pitmaster during a lull in that pit's matches. Dara started toward him, but a sound caught her attention—cruel, mocking laughter, distinct from the tumult. She stopped short at the edge of a nearby pit between two kneeling spectators, only a few yards from where Tamir was negotiating.

Dara looked down and saw a gladiator grinning below a crested helmet that concealed the top half of his face. He wore a steel breastplate, but his sinewy arms and legs were bare and glistening with sweat.

He was savagely battering a downed opponent, delivering ruthless kicks to the man's ribs. With each blow, the victim curled tighter, driven relentlessly across the pit floor, sliding helplessly over the gravel.

Numbed by the senseless violence, she heard Tamir ask, "Can you point me toward the worst fighter here?"

"What kind of foolish question is that?" the pitmaster responded gruffly.

"It is just my... *niece* here has gotten it into her head that she wants to try her hand at pit fighting."

The gladiator below her was obviously toying with his victim now, purposefully dragging out the merciless beating. Dara glanced toward Tamir just in time to see the pitmaster look at her dubiously, and she felt her ire begin to rise.

"You can't be serious," he said. "That little thing won't last a single match with these savages. If you're desperate for coin, she'd be better off hawking her wares in the Whisper Walk, with the rest of the alley-maidens. She's a lot easier on the eyes than most of that lot. Ought to be able to turn you a profit fast."

"Beast! Beast! Beast!" cried the onlookers above the pit beside her. Dara glanced down again as the dominant fighter seized his barely conscious opponent by the hair and dragged him into a kneeling position. He stood behind the wounded man, sword pressed to his throat. Then he looked up at the rim of the pit, nodding and grinning at the crowd.

She watched in horror as the victor slowly slashed open the kneeling man's throat, crimson spraying across the sand before him.

Dara glanced back at Tamir again.

"How dare you, sir?" he said indignantly to the pitmaster. "You insult the honor of both my niece and myself."

"Tamir!" she called.

He was preoccupied with his scolding of the pitmaster, however.

She looked back at the pit as two men with shaven heads, wearing only loincloths, descended the stone ladder. They quickly gathered up the corpse of the loser and passed him to two other men at the top, before climbing the ladder again themselves. The corpse was carried to the edge of the wall surrounding the crevice and tossed unceremoniously into the hidden depths below.

The winner had his fist in the air, spinning slowly as he took in the admiration from the heartless spectators. The air was charged with electricity, and Dara tasted the tang of salt and oiled steel.

"Tamir!" she called again.

He heard her finally and turned.

"This is the one," she said, pointing toward the gladiator in the pit below her. "I can forgive myself if it comes down to him or me."

A perplexed look crossed Tamir's face. He turned to the pitmaster again, but Dara didn't wait for her mentor to acknowledge if he understood her intention. She needed to act before she lost her resolve.

She took a deep breath and jumped down to the sandy floor of the pit.

The man standing before her in the steel breastplate and helmet towered over her, at least six and a half feet tall.

Dara swallowed. She looked around quickly, then up. The edge of the pit loomed a full yard over her opponent's head.

Nāb al-Sahra's exultant laughter echoed against the back of her skull.

Her adversary grinned, reading the fear in her eyes. He dropped his bloody sword and slowly picked up a trident. Wordlessly, he came at her.

She whipped the scimitar from its scabbard and swatted away the trident. Rolling to his right side, she came to her feet behind him.

"Look out, child!" Tamir warned from above.

Her foe was on her again. She repeated the maneuver as before, but this time he anticipated it, swatting her legs from beneath her with the blunt end of the trident.

Dara's shoulder collided with the wall of the pit. She recovered in time to avoid the deadly tines of the trident as it was thrust at her, and made a run for the ladder. Better to escape and come up with a new plan to rid herself of the sword.

"Fool," Nab al-Sahra's harsh whisper stabbed into her mind. *"No matter. I will soon claim another. One who will serve me without question."*

As she neared the ladder, she heard laughter above and watched in horror as the pit wranglers upended wicker baskets, dropping dozens of snakes into the pit. She skidded to a halt before the hissing, writhing mass of cobras, their bodies banded with red, orange, and black stripes.

She turned just in time to meet another thrust of the trident, and an exchange of blows followed in rapid succession. The clangor of steel echoed in the pit as the combatants began to circle each other.

Dara knew she was outmatched. Her adversary knew it too. He flexed his muscles in a show of dominance, and the crowd above cheered.

One of the cobras slithered between her feet then, straight toward her opponent. Seeing its approach, a startled look crossed his face, but instead of retreating, he speared it with his trident and flung it aside with a quick flick of the weapon.

He laughed and rushed her straight on. When she parried this time, he trapped her blade in the fork of the trident and forced the tip of her sword to the sandy floor. Using the long handle of the trident like a pole, he leaped and kicked her solidly in the chest.

Dara landed hard, sliding across the floor toward the snakes. She was dazed but managed to keep her grip on the scimitar.

Over the sound of her ragged breathing, she heard the heavy footsteps of her foe and saw the shadow of the raised trident looming above her. But her face was turned away from him as she stared into the eyes of the closest viper.

"Beast! Beast! Beast!" chanted the crowd.

Despite the pain, her eyes narrowed. Time seemed to slow. Something was off about the vipers. Their markings weren't red, orange, and black like the Katili cobra Tamir had once shown her in an illustration. No—these snakes bore red, black, and orange bands.

A sudden memory stirred—her five- or six-year-old self, digging a hole beside her family's hut in Besh. A snake just like these had slithered up through the dirt. She'd screamed, but her mother had chided her. It was only an Aithris viper, harmless except for the sting of its bite.

"Stupid wench," her murderous adversary gloated, savoring the moment before delivering the killing blow.

Dara rolled toward the Beast, ignoring the trident poised above her, and whipped her hand toward him. The viper flew upward and struck, sinking its fangs into his cheek.

He howled in pain, dropping the trident and clawing at the snake still clinging to his face.

Dara rose to a crouch and drove Nab al-Sahra into his guts from below, just beneath his breastplate. She tore it free as he sank to his knees.

Looming over him now, she said, "That snake wasn't venomous. Now who's stupid?" She swung the sword, and his helmeted head rolled across the floor of the pit.

There was a stunned silence above.

Dara looked at the black opal in the pommel and saw the spectral eye staring back at her.

"Yesss!" Nab al-Sahra hissed. *"I underestimated you. But this is only the beginning. The streets of Thiardun will run red!"*

An almost overwhelming euphoria bloomed in her chest, spreading to her limbs like a rolling storm.

The wranglers jumped into the pit with hook-staves and wicker baskets and began gathering the snakes.

Tamir appeared at the top of the ladder, his face full of concern. The sight of him bolstered her defiance like a dam straining to hold back a wave of blissful domination that sought to subvert her will—but the cracks were already forming.

She ran toward him. "Get back! Clear the way!"

"What are you doing?" the demon roared as Dara reached the ladder.

She climbed it one-handed, pushing her mentor out of her way and running toward the wall that surrounded the crevice. She could feel cold, barbed claws digging into her mind, injecting rage into her thoughts.

Dara fell to her knees, clutching at the low wall with her free hand. Something unseen squeezed her fingers against the hilt until her knuckles turned white. Fire coursed through her veins. Her sword arm began to seize.

"You are mine!" Nab al-Sahra howled. *"Obey me, and the world will tremble at your feet!"*

She hurled the cursed blade into the abyss. It spun through the air, its silent scream piercing her ears, the black opal catching one last glint of light before vanishing into the deep.

Dara felt hands at her arm. Tamir helped her rise slowly to her feet, a look of cautious uncertainty on his face.

"You are free," he said—the words more a question than a statement.

Tamir suddenly collided with her, nearly sending them both over the wall surrounding the fissure.

Dara closed her eyes tightly, holding her breath and anticipating the unbidden surge of anger and madness.

But it didn't come.

She opened her eyes and saw what had nearly sent them headlong into the crevice. It was Kephius, the high priest of Sibilee, and his eunuch bodyguards shoving spectators out of the way to clear a path as they swept past toward one of the pits on the far side of the vault.

The priest was heavily adorned with gold and jewels.

Dara wiped the sweat from her brow and smiled at Tamir.

His face flooded with relief, and he embraced her. He started to speak, then stopped himself.

It didn't matter. She already knew what he wanted to say. He wanted to tell her it was time to change her ways and leave behind the dangerous life of a thief.

She smiled again, looking back at the hypocritical priest. Perhaps Tamir was right. She did need to change her ways—*but not today.*

ABOUT THE AUTHOR

Guy Stapp is a lifelong fan of fantasy, horror, and sword & sorcery fiction. Originally from California, he served four years in the U.S. Army before settling in Florida, where he lived for more than three decades. He now resides in Arizona.

His love of the genre began in childhood, sparked by the fantasy writings of Lloyd Alexander, stoked by Dungeons & Dragons and the original theatrical releases of *Conan the Barbarian* and *The Beastmaster*, and deepened through the works of Robert E. Howard, Fritz Leiber, and H.P. Lovecraft. His writing draws from that same tradition, blending high-stakes heroism with creeping dread and ancient evils.

Steel Against the Damned is his debut collection.

For updates on future releases, visit:

www.urganothpress.com

COMING SOON

And the Damned Shall Bleed

Book Two of *The Damned*

www.ingramcontent.com/pod-product-compliance
Lightning Source LLC
Chambersburg PA
CBHW020912310726
48980CB00011B/851/J

* 9 7 9 8 9 9 4 0 6 8 2 2 9 *